The Ga[...]

Gate 1
Fantasy

Wren Havyn

Copyright © 2021 Wren Havyn

All rights reserved. No part of this book may be reproduced or used in any manner without the prior written permission of the copyright owner,
except for the use of brief quotations in a book review.

To request permissions, contact the publisher at thegatekeepersshop@gmail.com.

Paperback: 978-0-578-32344-2

Fourth paperback edition November 2021.

To my TikTok followers:
If it weren't for your love and support this book would not exist.
Thank you.

Lustria

- The Gateway
- Grasslands
- Celestial Beach
- Valkravine
- Dwarves
- Crystal Caves

The hideout
Her lair
Kygra's Island
The Tower
The Great Tree
Luma
Brendalwyn
Wishing Well
Flower Fields
Laqmirth
Elves
Pass
The Plains
Misthold
The Staircase
Elyra the Stoneless
Sparkling Pool
Fairy Glen
Unicorn Haven

If you are expecting this book to have a satisfying ending I would kindly ask that you change those expectations now.

In fact, when you reach the last page of this book, I can guarantee you will have more questions than answers, for this is a book of beginnings. Then why even begin? You ask. Ah, but even the world's greatest adventures have to start somewhere. Am I saying that this is going to be one of the world's greatest adventures? That I will let you decide for yourself. But what if magic, the kind you only see on tv or read in books, the kind you wished with all your heart to be real, actually existed? If you find yourself intrigued by this statement, then, may I suggest, you begin...

Chapter 1

I took the skeleton key hanging around my neck and opened the secret compartment in my apothecary's chest. A hidden box jumped up and I pulled out a small leather pouch from it. I ran out the door of my apartment and hopped into my car, fumbling with the leather straps of the pouch as I tied it around my waist.

I quickly drove through the little American town I had grown up in, which wasn't anything noteworthy... except for the secret it possessed.

My car finally skidded to a stop in the overgrown dirt parking lot hidden off one of the back roads at the far end of town. I stared into the dense forest before me. My heart pounded with excitement; gatekeeper meetings were my favorite. I quickly jumped out, and instead of taking the overgrown old hiking trail marked with a rusty sign, I headed in the opposite direction and ducked through a curtain of vines overhanging a cluster of gigantic boulders. I made my way through a short tunnel and emerged on the other side, the air mysteriously feeling much cooler. I followed the faint path that now stretched out in front of me.

I unhooked the leather pouch I had at my waist, opened it up, and pulled out a clear diamond-shaped gemstone, which had begun to thrum. I smiled and sped up my pace. Eventually, the forest opened up into a large clearing. A circular stone platform sat in the open space, and on it were twelve stone archways, all in a circle and facing the center, where a stone pedestal with a bowl on the top stood. It looked like a more organized version of Stonehenge. Each of the archways had a circular cutout at the top which contained a pane of glass. These panes of glass varied in color, each gate having its own unique hue.

As usual, I was the first to arrive. I stepped onto the platform and watched as the gemstone in my hand lit up and turned a light blue. I simultaneously felt a familiar space open up in my mind, the place where all my magical abilities were organized and available for me to access. I used my magic to perform a quick light orb in the palm of my hand. It was an exhilarating experience, one I craved every time I was away from it. With a quick jerk of my hand, I made the orb disappear and put the stone back in its pouch, the magic in my mind faded as my fingers left its smooth surface.

    I walked to the center of the circle and dipped my hand into the stone bowl, which contained hundreds of smaller multi-colored gemstones. The colors all correspond with the different colored glass above the archways. The coolness of all the tiny stones felt satisfying against my fingers. Typically, these stones would be glowing, powered by the magic inside of them just like my larger gatekeeper's stone in my pouch. Instead, they were dark and cold. I took a moment to look through them, seeing if I could find a rare clear stone. When I couldn't find any, I turned and made my way towards the head of the circle where the biggest archway stood above the rest on its own platform. This gate's pane of glass was colorless, just like the tiny gemstone I had just attempted to find. I walked up the steps leading to it and sat down in its shade. I felt like I had just leaned my head back against it and closed my eyes when I suddenly heard the gate directly across from me come to life. The crimson-colored glass at the archway's peak began to glow, and with a swoosh, a swirling crimson-tinted portal appeared within the archway. A moment later, Grayson, a tall, bright blonde-haired boy my age, stepped through. He was the mysterious type and always seemed to be up to something. He walked around with his hands in his pockets most of the time too, like he was posing for a photoshoot. People that are hard to read make me feel uneasy and he was definitely one of those people. I stayed very still, hoping to avoid the inevitable awkward conversation we would have if he did see me.

He casually walked to the center of the circle, took one of his hands out of his pocket, and waved it in front of him, causing a round stone table to appear around the pedestal with the gemstones. With another wave of his hand, twelve chairs appeared. He abruptly put his hand back in his pocket and sat down in the chair closest to him. To my relief, other gatekeepers started arriving and sitting at the seats in correspondence with their realm. I eventually stood up and joined them.

After a moment, Trez, our leader from the Pirate realm, spoke up, "Looks like we are all here. Let's get started then." He took off his pirate hat and set it on the table. He should have kept it on; his hair was a mess. "Alright, welcome everyone. As the first order of business, it seems that gate three has a new gatekeeper. Would you mind introducing yourself?"

I looked over to my left, shocked I hadn't noticed the small girl who sat in the mermaid realm's chair. The new gatekeeper sat there fidgeting nervously. She had long flowing blonde hair and the face of a goddess, which was currently bright red.

"My name is Isla," she squeaked. "Gatekeeper Rena has stepped down and has kindly offered the position to me."

Grayson scoffed, and I knew why. We all knew Rena and she wasn't one to "step down". There must have been an overthrow of power, which often happened in the Mermaid realm.

"Thank you, Isla, and welcome to the gatekeepers. My name is Trez, gatekeeper to realm eight, the Pirate realm, and these are your fellow gatekeepers." He gestured to everyone at the table. "To kill two birds with one stone, I will let them introduce themselves when we go around and give realm reports."

She nodded her head to show she understood but seemed distracted. Trez was about to continue, but she spoke up before he could begin. "Are those more gate keys?" she pointed to the bowl in the center of the table. We all stared at her.

"Yes, but they currently do not possess any power," Trez said after a moment's pause.

Usually, when new gatekeepers came to meetings, they at least had some idea of what being a gatekeeper entailed, but this poor girl seemed to know absolutely nothing. It made me wonder what actually happened to Rena.

"What? Why don't they have any power?" Isla forgot her timidity for a moment, sounding more like a person than a mouse.

"Well, long ago, when Linore came from The Gate of Light," Trez gestured toward the gate I had been sitting under, "she created the other eleven realms for the people of The Dim, or the real world as Wren calls it, to come and experience magic. Linore created these stones to grant the user access to the corresponding realm, according to the color of the gemstone."

Isla nodded her head, listening intently.

"One day, Linore cut the magical power from these stones so that no one else could enter the realms, and she disappeared. However, the gate keys still continue to reproduce inside this basin, but they now contain no magical abilities whatsoever. They are essentially useless."

Isla sank back into her seat, looking defeated.

"But don't worry Isla," I chimed in, "We have been working on finding Linore so we can get the power back to the gemstones. Rena told me that your realm struggles with not having enough working gemstones, which is also an issue in my realm. So we think if we get all the gatekeeper stones together, we can somehow summon Linore." I waved my hand at the other gatekeepers. "But as you can see, we have a few gatekeepers still missing. Hopefully, we can find them soon."

Isla's eyes lit up. "Really? That would be wonderful!"

"Do you have any further questions, Isla?" asked Trez.

She started to shake her head but then stopped. "Oh, um, yes, actually. I do have one more thing, but I think I already know the answer. I, uh, was told I had to ask if you have any more gemstones of light, you know, the clear-colored gate key gemstones that give you more power?"

At first, no one said anything. It was a bold and rude thing to just ask for, considering they were so rare and valuable.

"Sorry, Isla, we don't have any extras," I finally said, knowing full well that none of the other gatekeepers were willing to give up any they had. "They are so rare that I don't think there are any in the gate key pedestal."

Isla blushed. "Ok, I am sorry. Thank you, though, for answering. I am done asking questions now!" she squeaked and then sunk back into her chair.

"Well, alright then," said Trez, stretching. "Let's get right into introductions and reports then, shall we? As per usual, Wren, you go first and be sure to introduce yourself."

I nodded. "Hi Isla, my name is Wren, and I am the gatekeeper for gate one, the fantasy realm. It's full of dwarves, elves, unicorns, fairies, and wizards and has some of the most beautiful scenery to exist, full of sparkling waterfalls, rolling hills, and endless fields of flowers. I also get to stay in an amazing castle that is located on top of one of those waterfalls. But when I am not there, I actually live in the real world, or The Dim as you call it. So I have someone run my realm for me when I am gone, and his name is Falveron. As for my update, Falveron is still concerned about the low number of working gate key gemstones in the realm. The elves have already come to the capital to demand more gemstones, and I am sure the dwarves are not far behind," I turned to Isla. "So just like in your realm, where you need a working gate key gemstone to become a mermaid, we need them in ours if you want to become an elf or a dwarf. When someone is born in the elf or dwarf cities, and they don't have enough gate keys, they stay a human, and neither the dwarves nor elves are too happy about that," I turned back to the rest of the group and smiled. "But other than that, things are going great."

"Thank you, Wren," Trez said. "Next."

Launch, sitting directly to my left, put his headphones down around his neck and ran his hand through his messy brown hair to try to smooth it down, which really didn't help. He was the most normal looking out of all the gatekeepers, at least to me. He always wore sweatpants and a hoodie.

"Hi, uh, my name is Launch. I am the gatekeeper to gate two, the space realm. We all live on a space station called Atmos. Most people in my realm are avid gamers, but some like me go exploring, especially to the few surrounding planets that we have," He awkwardly paused and then continued. "So for my update, I, umm, have been working on a few things, and one of those things is potentially finding a way into the unknown realms."

Silence filled the circle. Trez shifted in his seat. "Well, this is quite the news. How close are you to achieving this?"

"Well, I have set up the engine core in my ship to take the energy from the sun stones and convert it into a field that disrupts the outer core of my realm, allowing me to break through and enter the void."

"The void?" asked Trez, furrowing his brows.

"Yes, the space where all the realms reside."

Silence filled the circle once again. Launch usually went into rants about different things he was working on, but most of the time, we never knew what to believe.

"I see," said Trez, who clearly didn't.

"The only issue I have now is obtaining enough energy to break through multiple realm walls so I can safely make it back to my realm. It will take a few more months, so I will keep you all posted on how that is going."

"Alright," said Trez, "Sounds good. We look forward to hearing more."

I was super intrigued by what Launch was saying, but since I didn't fully understand it, I didn't ask any further questions. Launch was always working on odd projects and at this point, we just learned that it was best to wait till he had something to actually show for it.

"Ok, Isla, let's move on to you. Anything else to report from your realm?"

Isla turned bright red again and shook her head.

"Ok," Trez said, "that is fine, Fynne?"

Fynne scratched his orange beard and straightened his ornate tunic. "Hello, Isla, my name is Fynne, and I am the gatekeeper to gate four, the medieval realm. I am the head knight in my realm, but ultimately our realm is run by the king and queen. I also have a family, my wife Joan and my three kids, which I would love for you to meet someday," He smiled. "As for my update. We are still having trouble with the witch I have mentioned in the past," He turned back to Isla. "There is a woman in our realm that has been cursing individuals with random disabilities." He explained to her, "She hasn't been seen in a while, but she made an appearance just last week. She cursed a child with blindness during the day but can see at night. Random, I know, but that is what this witch is known for. She has been a plague on our land since before I was born. I have sent out scouting parties to try and locate her but she seems to elude us every time. Besides that, there is nothing new to report."

"I am sorry to hear that. Please continue to keep us posted about the witch. Also, if there is anything we can do to help, let us know," said Trez.

Fynne nodded.

"Well, as you can see, Isla, we don't have a gatekeeper for gate five, which is currently one of the unknown realms. So that brings us to Grayson."

As usual, Grayson looked completely bored with this whole meeting but sat up from slouching in his chair.

"My name is Grayson, and I am the gatekeeper of The Chasm." He paused.

I held my breath, thinking he may actually share more information this time. As far as I was concerned, Grayson's realm was also an unknown realm because he never talked about it.

"And I have nothing to report," he finally said. Via, who was sitting a couple of chairs to my right, groaned. I looked at her and rolled my eyes.

"Grayson is the only other person who lives in the Dim, like Wren," said Trez, who I could tell was also slightly annoyed.

Isla nodded her head.

"Alright, moving along," Trez nodded towards Jumana. She was a petite older woman with long jet black hair. She wore a gold-trimmed blue sari. She looked to be in her early 50's, but she had once told me she was over 200 years old. With the amount of wisdom she possessed, it made sense.

"Hello Isla, my name is Jumana, and I am the gatekeeper to realm seven, the desert realm," she said in a calming voice. "You are always welcome to visit my realm to have some tea if you ever need someone to talk to. The desert realm air really helps to clear the mind. As for an update, we are doing very well," she turned to the rest of the group. "My Great Great Great Granddaughter, Yara, just took her first steps the other day. And she did them when coming to me. Her mom was very jealous." chuckled Jumana, her eyes shining with pride. If only life in my realm was that simple and peaceful. "Other than that, there are no new updates. Things are peaceful as usual."

"Glad to hear," Trez smiled. "Alright, as you already know, my name is Trez, and I am the gatekeeper for gate eight, the pirate realm. As for my update, the Stalking Albatross has made another attempt to retake the gatekeeper's stone but failed miserably. They are more annoying than anything. Dark Waters and The Waning Moon, our rivals, have left us alone for the time being, which has been a nice break."

Isla shuffled in her seat. This girl must not get out much to seem terrified at just the mention of pirates crews she has never even heard of.

"My chief mate Riggs and I have been busy fortifying Skull Bay where our gate is located, and so far, everything has held up swimmingly."

I noticed Grayson roll his eyes. Guess he wasn't much for puns.

Trez didn't notice and continued, "That's it for me, nothing much else to report. So next we skip gate nine, another unknown realm. Then lastly we have Via."

I hadn't realized, but Via was practically upside down in her chair, lounging like a bored cat. She quickly sat up and spoke in a very fake British accent. It was her way of sounding professional. No one had the guts to tell her it was actually making her sound the opposite.

"Thank you, fearless leader Trez," she said as she stood up. She paused for effect and obnoxiously cleared her throat, "My name is Via, the youngest and most brilliant of the gatekeepers." I laughed out loud and immediately cuffed my hand over my mouth. Via continued without missing a beat, "My realm is the steampunk realm, a world full of beautiful and wondrous trinkets and mechanisms. If you ever visit, be prepared to have thou mind art blown." Her combination of the modern lingo I had been teaching her and the Shakespearean she loved to read was riveting. "To continue, in my most recent meeting with the Torian counsel, we discussed the low supply of slug leaf tea and Lord Ogden's cat, who had a terrible furball the other day. But do not worry yourselves. The cat is doing quite fine and did not succumb to death." At that, she sat back down in her chair and crossed her legs as if she just overtook a kingdom and was now sitting on their throne. Isla looked confused.

"Is that it?" said Trez with his eyebrows raised. I was just sitting there wondering if cats can actually die from a hairball.

Via crossed her arms and stuck her chin up in the air, "I am quite finished."

Trez shook his head, "Moving on."

Via leaned over towards me and loudly whispered, "How was that? I practiced it forever!" I gave her a thumbs up and winked. Poor Via never really had anything important to report. In her realm, she was more of a mascot than anything else. The Torian Counsel were the ones who governed the realm, a group of quirky old men in top hats, so wrapped up in their own business they didn't really care about what happened outside of the realm.

Trez cleared his throat. "Anyway, after Via is gate eleven, which is also an unknown gate, and then we come to gate twelve, the main gateway to all magic."

Isla nodded her head. "Well, nice to meet you all," she squeaked out.

"And you as well," said Trez. "I know it's a lot to take

in for your first meeting, and becoming a gatekeeper can be intimidating, but just know we are here if you ever need help. We are all just a message away." He said, motioning to her gatekeeper's stone on the elaborate headpiece that pressed against her forehead. She looked confused but didn't say anything.

I leaned toward Isla. "Did they ever teach you how to communicate with your gatekeeper's stone?"

"To do what?" she said, embarrassed.

"Here, let me show you," I said as I pulled my gemstone from its pouch again. "Ok, so all you need to do is form a message in your head and then send it to the gatekeeper you wish to send the message to. The easiest way for me to do it is to imagine sending the message to the gatekeeper's gemstone, specifically its color. So, for example, I am going to imagine sending a message to you by thinking of your teal gatekeeper's stone." I closed my eyes and sent "Hello, this is Wren."

Isla watched as my gemstone briefly turned from its light blue color to the teal color of her realm. Her gatekeeper's stone did the opposite. Her eyes opened wide as she received the message in her mind.

"Alright, how about you give it a try? Just imagine this light blue gemstone and send it a message."

To my surprise, she successfully sent me a message on her fourth try.

"Great job!" I said. "Ok, everyone, could you show Isla

your gatekeeper stones, so she knows what color belongs to who?"

Everyone brought their stones out, and I marveled at how pretty they looked sitting around the table, a rainbow of colors. I had Isla practice sending messages to each gatekeeper and watched as each of the stones lit up with Isla's teal color one by one. We went around the circle starting with Launch's darker blue stone, then to Fynne's Emerald green stone. We even practiced with Grayson and his dark red stone, a color I had never seen my stone turn because, obviously, he never sent any messages. We finished up with Jumana's yellow stone, Trez's bright red stone, and Via's purple stone. Launch began to practice sending messages to different people as well because he hadn't done it in a while, and before I knew it, everyone was sending each other messages. Isla even broke out laughing at one point.

Just as I was getting sick of hearing Via's voice in my head constantly repeating the words "doo doo," Trez finally spoke up. "Sorry to cut this short, but I have several things I need to attend to in my realm, so if no one has anything further statements or questions, I am going to get going." No one did, so we adjourned the meeting.

Via came running up to me. "Way to teach magic, Wren!" She gave me a high five. "Root has told me some stories of how badly magic training has been going with you, and I am impressed Isla made it out of your tutelage without a scratch."

She was clearly over-exaggerating, I had only set my friend Root on fire once, and he was fine.

"Who is Root?" came a voice from behind me. I turned around and came face to face with Grayson.

Chapter 2

I usually just observed Grayson's glaring face across the table, but now he was standing right in front of me. He seemed even more menacing closer up. I took a step back.

"Root is the son of the captain of the guard in my realm. He is my personal guard and trainer when it comes to magic." I said, hoping he would just leave.

"The man speaks!" Via said, being her overdramatic self. I punched her shoulder. Grayson stood there, unamused.

"Could I visit your realm sometime?"

"What?" His blunt question caught me off guard.

"I would like to check out your realm," He repeated. I looked back at Via, who seemed just as shocked as I was.

"Umm... Well, let me ask Falveron."

"That would be great."

"Cool, well, uh, I am actually headed to my realm now, and I will talk to Falveron when I am there. He will probably say yes, but I'll let you know what he says."

"Awesome. In that case, I am going to give you my phone number. Then you can let me know what he says, and we can plan a time for me to come if he says yes." He began to pull out his phone from his pocket.

"What about our stones?" I said.

"Our stones don't work in the real world, remember?"

"Oh, yeah, of course."

We awkwardly exchanged numbers.

"Cool, thanks, see you," he said as he snapped his fingers, which caused the table in the center of the gate circle to vanish. He jumped off the gate circle platform and disappeared into the woods. I just stood there flabbergasted until I felt Via grab my arm and shake it.

"What was that?" She yelled.

"I don't know! I can't believe I forgot my stone only works once I make it to the gate circle. And why didn't I ask why he wanted to come into my realm in the first place?"

I groaned and covered my face with my hands.

"I thought he had a thing for you, but watching him ask to come to your realm was like watching paint dry," said Via. "He didn't even seem nervous. I am questioning my insight on these matters."

"Via, you're 14, what do you know of these matters?"

"Oh, plenty," said Via, " I am very intuitive when it comes to people. It's how I basically won the gatekeeper's stone."

She had a point.

"Whatever," I said. "Besides, it's pretty clear that he basically hates everyone."

"I don't know about that," replied Via. Before she could continue, I heard Isla's tiny voice say my name.

"Wren?" she said. I turned around to face her. "I just wanted to say that I am very glad you are trying to find the woman who can supply the gate keys with power again. If there is ever anything I can do to help, just let me know."

"It's no problem at all!" I responded. "And the same goes for you. If you ever need anything or have any questions, just let me know. I know becoming a gatekeeper can be intimidating at first, but you'll get the hang of it."

"Thank you," she said as her eyes pooled. "That means a lot to me."

"Is everything ok?" I asked, concerned. It would be nice if she confirmed my theory about Rena being overthrown, but I didn't want to upset her further either.

"Oh yes," she said, blinking away the tears. "My eyes get watery when I am out of the water for too long, so I should probably go back. Thanks again." Without waiting for a response, she darted back to her gate, struggled for a minute to open it, and then awkwardly dove into it.

"That's a little sus," said Via.

"You are completely right," I said, proud of her successful use of the word sus, which I taught her last week. "Something is definitely going on in the mermaid realm. I hope Rena is doing ok."

"I was thinking the same thing," sighed Via. "Isla seems pretty cool, though. We should just try being her friend, and then maybe one day she will feel comfortable telling us what's going on."

"Sounds like a good plan. Well, I am headed to my realm now to check in. Would you like to come with me?"

"I totally wish I could, but Mr. Hopperkins needs my help repairing his dirt extractor, and then the lords need me at some party they are throwing. But maybe next time!"

I hugged Via and waved goodbye as she skipped through her gate, disappearing into her realm's portal.

I turned around and grabbed my stone. The rush of my magical abilities once again flooded my mind. I placed my hand on the stone archway and accessed the ability to open it. I felt the click of the gate opening and watched as the light blue glass at its peak lit up, and a thin film of misty blue light filled the archway. It was so mesmerizing to watch the color of my realm swirl behind a water-like barrier. But the best part of it all was stepping through it into my realm. It felt as if you'd landed face-first into a vat of jello that sucked you in and popped you out the other side but with less jello and more magic.

The view that greeted me as I emerged out the other side

always took my breath away. The gate opened up at the highest point, from which you could see the entire island that made up my realm, Lustria. All the way to the mist billowing up from the elven bay city of Misthold in the east to the dwarves stronghold of Valkravine in the mountains to the south. Behind me were steep cliffs that led down into an ocean surrounding our island that smelled of fresh water and sunshine. Directly in front of me was the flat grassy plateau that the gate was located on. Beyond that was a steep, rocky decline that led down into the capital city of my realm, which was called Luma. I took a moment to soak it all in, allowing the cool, fresh air to fill my lungs.

I took a deep breath. It was so quiet and peaceful, which made me remember that usually, Root met me at the gate, but he was nowhere to be seen. I must have arrived early, which filled me with excitement. Being on my own was rare in my realm, so I wanted to make the most of this moment. I crossed the grassy plateau and made my way down the long winding path to Luma. On my way, I passed the large abandoned watchtower and briefly stopped at the blueberry patch to get a quick snack. I finally made it to Luma's outskirts, a bustling port city that sat at the edge of the bay. I made my way through the crowds, people occasionally stopping to say hello and children asking to see my gatekeeper's stone.

Suddenly, someone jumped out of the alley I was passing and yelled "Wren!"

I closed my eyes, screamed, and crouched down in the

fetal position. A familiar laugh met my ears. I opened my eyes and found Root standing there, his pointy ears sticking out of his bouncing curly orange hair. I stood up and punched him in the arm.

"Root! Why do you always do that?"

"Because your reactions are priceless," Root was still chuckling to himself, "And watch it! You'll crease the uniform!" He brushed his navy blue uniform where I'd punched him.

I rolled my eyes.

"Also, why didn't you tell me you were coming early! It's my job to meet you at the gate and walk you into town. You know my father won't be too happy about this either."

"Oh Root, it's fine! It's only half an hour's walk. And nothing bad has ever happened in the past year since I got here."

"I'll let it go this once," he replied. "But next time, please let me know."

"Yes, sir," I said, saluting.

"So you off to see Falveron?"

"Well, that's usually what I do when I visit," I said sarcastically. I made my way through the busy streets as Root kept up with me. "What else would I be doing?"

"Getting into trouble, accidentally lighting something on fire, talking to a cow thinking it could talk back, the possibilities are endless, really." he quipped.

"How was I supposed to know when I first arrived that

cows couldn't talk anyway? It's a magical place, and talking cows just made sense."

"There, there." He patted my head.

I smirked at him and dramatically brushed his hand away. Pretending to be mad at him was a game we played often. I walked faster.

"Aw, common Wren," said Root, running to catch up. He passed me, stopped, and bowed directly in front of me. "Your majesty, your humble servant apologizes for bringing up such a painful and humiliating memory. How can I ever repay you for such negligence? Please, tell me!" He was causing a scene, and several people started to stare.

"You can start by stopping this nonsense!" I whispered harshly as I tried to get him to stop bowing at me. He resisted for a while, smiling at the lack of progress I was making, and then abruptly straightened up.

"Yes, milady, anything for you milady." He turned on his heel, grabbed my hand, placed it on his arm, and began officially escorting me to the castle.

"That's not fair," I whined. "You always one-up me by embarrassing me."

"When will you ever learn," he responded in a fake gentleman's accent. "You have no idea the talent I possess, and that's what makes you weak."

He twisted himself out of my grasp on his arm but then immediately bumped into someone. "Father! I mean captain!"

Root promptly saluted.

"Root," His father responded sternly. Root's father was intimidating at first, but I appreciated it because he was the captain of the guard. I always felt completely safe when he was around because I knew he would never let anything bad happen to me. He was every bit as loyal as Root was, if not more. "Falveron has heard of Wren's arrival and needs to see the both of you immediately."

"Yes, Captain Tarren," replied Root, regaining composure. "We are headed there now." He saluted once again.

"Good to see you again, Wren," said the captain as Root and I passed him. He had changed his tone of voice and was smiling at me. Even though Captain Tarren was intimidating, he also knew when to be gentle and kind.

"You too, captain. Thank you!" I said as we ran off toward the castle.

I could hear the waterfall before I could even see the beautiful castle I called home. It was known as Bridgeway Castle because it acted as a bridge under which a small river ran and dropped off into a waterfall on the south side. There were many oddly placed turrets and courtyards, which added to its quirky splendor.

The guards let us through the large iron gates that opened up to the front courtyard. To our right and down a wide white stoned path were the stables, and directly in front of us, the path continued and circled in front of the great castle doors. Root and I made our way towards the castle, butterflies darting across our path and into the neatly kept shrubs and flowers that made up the front garden that filled the rest of the courtyard.

"I have to go get changed first," I said to Root as we entered the castle, and I started making my way towards the wing where my bedroom was. "Please tell Falveron I'll be there in a few minutes!"

"Yes, Milady," he said over exaggerating a bow.

I ran up the winding marble stairs, my steps echoing throughout the great castle. When I first came to the realm, Falveron insisted that I take the royal suite, but I refused. Sure, I was the gatekeeper, but Falveron was technically still running the realm, and it only felt right for him to stay. So instead, I chose this room that overlooked the waterfall. Falveron had it fitted with all the necessities I could ever need, including a wardrobe that fulfilled all my childhood princess dreams. I opened the ornate wooden door and was greeted with the scent of lavender and my handmaid Lyra. She had the ears of an elf but the stout build of a dwarf, a rare combination in our realm. She was also one of the sweetest people you would ever meet.

"Hello, miss!" she exclaimed when I entered my room. "I heard you had arrived, and I laid out a dress for you. Just slip that on, and I will do your hair right quick!"

I ran to my canopy bed, which was bigger than my entire bedroom back in the real world, and picked up the dress lying there. It was a beautiful light blue velvet dress with silver trimmings and long sleeves that swooped down to the floor. I quickly slipped it on and sat down at my dressing table where Lyra was fussing with a bottle of fairy wing dust.

"Sorry," she said, "I am having trouble getting this cork off."

"Here, let me help," I said, taking it from her hands.

"Thank you."

Fairy wing dust was used as a magic boost in our realm, much like the gemstones of light, yet it was more accessible and not as rare. In my realm, fairies shed their wings, which is why you would always see a shimmering trail behind every flying fairy. There were certain seasons that fairies would shed their wings more than usual, and the dust, as we called it, would collect in specific locations within Fairy Glenn. During these seasons, people would go down to Fairy Glenn and collect the dust to sell it in the market. It was very popular, especially because it could even be used for small, simple magic by people that didn't possess a gate key gemstone. Otherwise, it was used as a magic boost for those that did have a gate key gemstone, like Lyra.

I finally popped the cork off, and Lyra took a pinch and sprinkled it over my head. In seconds, my light brown hair turned into cascading waves, and my face was done up in simple but beautiful makeup. She then placed my gatekeeper's crown on my head. It was silver and shaped to look like a vine with flowers. Light blue gemstones made up the center of the flowers.

While she was working, she was able to quickly update me on the castles going ons and had just finished telling me about how one of the kitchen maids accidentally dropped a pie on one of the castle cats when there came a knock on the door. A porter announced that he was ready to escort me down the great hall, and I jumped up to follow him.

Falveron was already waiting for me, seated at the long narrow meeting table in the large decorated room. He was a shorter man, and like most people in my realm, including myself, stayed human when using his gate key gemstone, rather than turning into a dwarf or elf. He was decked out in elaborate robes and wore a crown to signify his place as a steward.

"Come in, come in," he said, waving at me to come over. "Please be seated."

I bowed to Falveron and took my place in the chair to his right. Root took his usual place next to me.

"Lord Falveron, it's good to see you." I smiled. "I trust everything is going well."

"Well, Wren, there have been some troubling news that

has come up since your last visit."

"Oh no, did something happen with Kygra? Did she attack the wood elf village?" I knew Root's extended family lived there, and Kygra, our resident Dragon, lived on an island just off the shore where the little wood elf village of Brendalwyn sat. It was always a concern that one day she might attack it.

"No, no, nothing like that. Kygra has not shown her face on the mainland and is still safe on her island. This is a matter with the dwarves and the elves concerning the gate key gemstones."

"Oh." This wasn't new news to me. We'd been talking about this for the past few months. "I know the elves have been asking for more working gemstones. And I have been working on finding Linore to get the power back to the gate keys in the pedestal, not that I have made much headway with that just yet. But I thought the knowledge of that to the elves would get them to calm down."

Flaveron scratched his thick brown beard. "Well, yes, that information pacified them for the moment, but now our issue is not just with the elves. The dwarf king Dorgan is here at this very moment, and he has heard of the elves' plea for more gemstones. He is furious and wants to speak with me right away. I was hoping to give him more information than we did the elves because, to be honest, they won't take that as an answer for long. That's why I wanted to meet with you right away, to figure out if you had made any headway on your search."

"Well, Gatekeeper Launch did have some encouraging news regarding getting into other realms today. He said he had made a discovery that might allow us to get into the unknown realms, but knowing Launch, I wouldn't put all my hope in that."

Falveron sighed. "Well, at least it's better than nothing. Would you mind joining us for dinner tonight and explaining it to the dwarf king himself?"

Suddenly the great hall doors flew open, and a very large gruff-looking man wearing a crown made with raw crystals bumbled in. Three guards were trying to stop him but to no avail.

Root leaned over to me and whispered, "Or you could just tell him now, I guess."

"Falveron," roared the dwarf. "How dare you keep me waiting! I demand we speak now!"

Chapter 3

"King Dorgan," said Falveron calmly. "Welcome. I thought we had discussed meeting over dinner."

"I made it clear that this was urgent, Falveron," growled the dwarf king. He turned to Root and me. "Who are these children that you have had to delay our meeting for?"

"This," said Falveron, "Is Wren, our gatekeeper. If I remember correctly, you politely refused to come to the celebration we had for her when she first arrived in our realm. In fact, you have declined every invitation I have sent for the past several years, so you complaining about a slight delay is a tad overreacting if you ask me." I could tell Root was trying to hold back a smirk.

The dwarf king briefly looked befuddled. "How dare you address me in such a way! And this little girl is our gatekeeper? What does she know of our world? You fools have no right wielding such power!" He started to make his way to where I was sitting. Before I could even react, Root jumped to his feet, drew his sword, and stood in between the dwarf king and me. The three guards that had followed him in also drew their swords, ready to charge.

"Enough!" Falveron stood up, his voice echoing across the room.

Everyone froze.

Falveron sat back down slowly. "King Dorgan, please have a seat, and we can begin our meeting now. There is no need for this, and I feel we can come to some sort of understanding."

The three guards slowly resheathed their swords, but Root still stood there, sword drawn.

King Dorgan looked Root up and down and scoffed. "If you think a scrawny elf-like yourself can stand up to someone like me, you are gravely mistaken."

Root said nothing, but I could tell he was fighting the urge to lunge at the dwarf king. Falveron cleared his throat.

King Dorgan smirked and made his way to his seat. It wasn't till the dwarf king sat down that Root sheathed his sword and did the same. My heart was pounding. I gave Root a grateful look. He did not look happy.

"Alright," said Falveron. "Now, King Dorgan, please share your concerns with us."

King Dorgan grunted. "I was told that the elves came to you and requested more gate key gemstones."

"This is true," said Falveron.

The dwarf king briefly looked like he was about to fly into a rage again but composed himself and continued, "And were they given any?"

"No, you know as well as I that we don't just have gate keys lying around. Most stones have been in families for generations. But we are working to come up with a solution." Falveron gestured to me.

"Oh yes," I said. "We do have more gate key gemstones in the pedestal in the gate circle, but unfortunately, they do not possess any power. But we believe that the original creator of the realms, Linore, can bring the power back to them. To do that, we first must find the three missing gatekeepers or, more specifically, their gatekeeper stones. Once we have all the stones together, we believe we can use them to summon her."

The dwarf king looked intrigued for a moment. "So, have you been searching for the stones in the realms?"

"Well, no, they are locked," I said bashfully.

"Then how do you plan on getting in to find the stones?" the dwarf king shouted. "What if the stones aren't even in there? Our stone spent twenty-five years outside of our realm!"

Root put his hand on the hilt of his sword. I started getting nervous again. "Well, you see, King Dorgan, one of my fellow gatekeepers may have found a way to enter those realms without the gatekeeper stones. And even if the gatekeepers live in the real worl... I mean, the Dim, like me, at least we can get in the realm and figure out what happened to them and see if we can get any further clues."

The dwarf king turned towards Falveron. "Is this really the best you got?"

"Yes," replied Falveron. "As I said, we do not have any extras we can spare, so the only other option is to wait and see what Wren and the fellow gatekeepers come up with."

The dwarf king leaned back in his chair. "You know that during the reign of my father, many of our gemstones were stolen, correct?"

"Yes," replied Falveron, "and according to my understanding, the thieves were never identified."

"Yes, that is right," said Dorgan. "And let me ask you, how many gemstones do the elves have in Misthold?"

"According to my knowledge, about eighty percent of the population has one."

The dwarf king tensed his jaw. "And do you know how many people have them in our city of Valkravine?" He clenched his teeth. "Ten percent, did you hear me, ten percent!" He slammed his fist on the table, making me jump. "I have had a hunch for years that the elves were the cause of our loss. I also noticed the amount of elves in Luma is high as well." He nodded at Root and suddenly stood up. "So here are my demands, you start collecting what is rightfully mine from those pointy-eared low lives or I may just have to start doing it myself. And I don't think you are going to approve of how I plan on doing it." He glared at Falveron, his eyes unwavering. "I will be back in twelve days' time to collect what is mine." With that, he stormed out of the great hall and slammed the door behind him.

The guard promptly apologized to Falveron and rushed after the dwarf king to make sure he didn't cause any more problems.

"Well, that was fun," said Falveron as he leaned on the table, head in his hand. My heart was still racing. I always thought the dwarves were peaceful, considering no one ever talked about them much, but I was clearly wrong.

"Are you ok, Wren?" Root asked from behind. I turned around and gave him a hug.

"Yes, I am fine," I stuttered. "I guess I just didn't realize how bad things were. I mean, I knew people were uneasy, but this is a whole other level I was not expecting."

"To be honest, I wasn't expecting that either," said Falveron. "The unfortunate thing is that there is not much to be done about the matter other than continuing your plan. The only other thing I could do is start demanding gemstones from people in Luma, but that would only cause more problems. And there is no way the elves would give some of their gemstones to the dwarves. But don't you worry, I will figure something out."

"Ok," I said, feeling completely useless. "In the meantime, I guess I will just need to ensure the gatekeepers know how serious this has become. I will bring it up in our next meeting. Trez seems to be the only other person who really wants to find Linore. Everyone else has their own stuff going on in their realms... Except for Grayson, which reminds me, Grayson wants to come to visit if that is ok." Both Root and Falveron suddenly looked up at me.

"You're joking, right?" asked Root. "We are talking about Grayson, the mysterious brooding guy you mention from your meetings. That Grayson?"

"Umm... yes, that's the one," I said.

"Well, what do you think, Wren?" asked Falveron.

I scratched my head. "Well, I think it should be ok, especially if Root is with me. For the most part, I feel like Grayson would be too lazy to cause any problems. He's been a part of our gatekeeper meetings and has never done anything. He seems pretty harmless. And him reaching out to visit other realms is a big deal. Maybe he is trying to connect with us more."

"Typical Wren," said Root. "Always thinking the best of people."

"And what's wrong with that?"

"Well, for starters, what if he, I don't know, tries to kill you?! And haven't you told me that gatekeepers can take their powers with them into other realms and obtain the power of that realm? If that's true, then we don't even know the power of his realm! It could be terrible!"

"First of all, you are being dramatic," I said. Root rolled his eyes. "And yes, he can indeed bring his powers with him into our realm but as far as I know, all he can do is make a table appear. That doesn't seem threatening to me. And if anything were to happen, you will be with me every step of the way to protect me." I smiled. "You could handle him if anything happens, right?"

Root looked at me as if to say, "really?"

Falveron spoke up, "Wren, I trust your judgment. If you are ok with Grayson coming to visit, then I am ok with it as well."

Root grunted.

"But you are right when you say that Root needs to be with you at all times. And please let me know when you plan on bringing him."

"Thank you, Falveron," I said. "If that is alright, I will bring him on my next weekly visit, the normal time."

"Don't I get a say in this?" Root complained.

"I know you are going to say yes to me anyway," I said, patting his back.

"I mean, you're not wrong," He mumbled.

"Well then that's settled," said Falveron. "And perhaps it will help him understand our situation a little bit better, get him on board to help us find Linore."

"True!" I said excitedly.

A porter appeared and announced dinner. My stomach growled at the thought of all the yummy realm food it was about to eat. The food here had flavors I couldn't even explain except that it was absolutely delicious. We made our way to the dining hall, where Falveron's family joined us. The table was stacked with all kinds of meats, salads, breads, and sides. But my personal favorite was the dessert, especially what they called cloud candy. It basically looked like cotton candy, but it instantly became chewy like a marshmallow when you first put it in your mouth. It would then randomly melt, sending a burst of what tasted like the smell of rain before a thunderstorm and a hint of strawberries through your mouth. It was weirdly amazing.

We finished up, and I went to bed. Something about my realm usually lulled me to sleep immediately, but tonight I lay in my bed staring out the window at the star-filled sky. Between almost dying and wondering if letting Grayson into my realm was a good idea, I tossed and turned for hours. The moment I felt like I had finally fallen asleep, I suddenly woke up to the sun streaming through my window and a loud pounding on my door.

"Wake up, sleepyhead!" said Root from the other side of the

door. "We have magic training to do and dragon scales to collect!"

Chapter 4

I loved magic training for obvious reasons. It's not every day you can practice creating a light orb or turning a rock into a frog. It also wasn't every day that you could go collect dragon scales.

    I dressed in my regular realm clothes, which consisted of tall leather boots, comfy trousers, a blouse, and a vest. Once I was dressed and ready, we headed off to our training grounds. After realizing the cramped horse yard at the castle was bad for magic training (especially after the "fire" incident), Root thought it best to find someplace more secluded. His solution was a large clearing located near his treehouse in the northeast woods. Root, being a wood elf, loved the outdoors, so when he was not working in Luma, he would stay in his self-constructed home in the Great Tree, the largest tree on the whole island.

The treehouse itself had several different rooms and levels, all connected by swinging bridges or ladders. The best part was the lookout located at the very top of the tree. Just like the view from the gate, you could see the whole island from there.

"Alright, let's get right into it, shall we?" said Root as we made it to the clearing. I quickly searched through my satchel to find my leather cuff. It was something that Root had made for me that kept my stone against the skin on my wrist. I pressed the flat top of my stone to the inside of my wrist and then wrapped and secured my cuff around it. The pointed end of my stone stuck through a hole in the cuff which made for a pretty good weapon in close combat.

We ran some mental exercises, the first of which included visualizing my abilities in my mind. Everyone's mind worked differently when it came to how you accessed your magical abilities. For example, Root said he imagined a long list of his abilities which he scrolled through to find and then perform. For me, I imagined all of my abilities were organized on shelves in a musty potion shop, each ability being a different potion on the shelf. All the shelves were labeled depending on the category of the magic. So there was one shelf labeled attack, another defense, another practical, and so on. All I had to do to perform an ability was to imagine myself drinking the potion, which locked in what I was going to cast. Once you hit that point, there was no going back.

I spent a moment perusing my "potions" to get my mind warmed up, and then we launched into our first exercise. I called it shelf jumping, which entailed me closing my eyes and then quickly performing whatever ability Root yelled at me while he did everything in his power to distract me. Today's distractions included little pebbles he threw at me, randomly tapping my shoulder, and the occasional dumping of water on my head. It wasn't my favorite, but I had to admit it really helped my concentration which was essential for good magic casting.

We then worked on a new ability to create a magic shield to block any magical attacks, which Root thought would be helpful if Grayson decided to try anything. All of my realms' abilities were there on my shelves, but I would have to dig around and find new ones so I could perform them. After a moment, I found the one labeled "Shield" and went to work attempting to perform it. For new abilities, I would start out saying the ability out loud to help me concentrate. Root would also walk me through what hand motions helped as well. Soon I was able to wave my hand in front of me, yell shield, and a temporary shimmering dome would appear around me.

Root then thought it would be a good idea to shoot fireballs at me to make sure it really worked. To my excitement, I was able to block them, but I accidentally sent one into a nearby tree, which then turned the whole situation into a refresher lesson on how to put out fire with magic.

To end magic training I always allowed Root to test out his abilities with my gatekeeper's stone. Since it was the gatekeeper's stone, it possessed more abilities and power than Root, even though he possessed a gate key gemstone and a gemstone of light. Since Root was my bodyguard, he was granted one of the four gemstones of light in our realm. The other three belonged to Falveron, Captain Tarren, and the elven queen. He kept both of these stones in a silver ring that kept them pressed against his finger. It was more practical than keeping them in the small glass jar necklaces that people usually wore.

Root practiced with his sword, using the gatekeeper's stone to light its blade on fire, one of the skills he didn't have with his normal stones. I watched as he stepped carefully around the clearing, swinging his flaming sword in quick, precise movements. He ended with one final slash upwards that caused a giant swirling tornado of fire to shoot up into the blue sky above. I sat there staring in awe as the warm breeze it created gently blew past my face. Root was definitely someone to contend with.

꧁꧂

After training was complete, It was time to head to Root's treehouse to pack up for our trip to collect dragon scales. As we were packing, I felt something bump my leg. I turned around, and Root's pet fox Neara was sitting there staring up at me. She pawed my leg again, clearly asking for a head rub. She let me pet her head once and then ducked away. Neara was probably the moodiest animal I have ever met but she seemed to finally be warming up to me. Our first encounter involved her attacking my leg and then biting my finger, so we clearly have come a long way. She mostly hung around the treehouse, and rarely did I see her in town. Root let her decide whether or not she would come with him when he went places and she seemed most comfortable staying home. But today, as we left, she decided she wanted to tag along.

  The three of us made our way west to where Root kept his small boat we used to sail over to Kygra's island. Sailing over didn't take long at all and we landed at the little dock near the hut Root had built for any overnight excursions. We trekked through the woods to the opposite side of the island where Kygra's cave was. It wasn't long before we arrived behind the giant boulder just before the mouth of the cave.

  Root motioned for me to be quiet and for Neara to sit. He poked his head around the boulder and soon motioned that the coast was clear. I took out my leather pouch to collect the scales and we quietly tiptoed into the cave. I immediately made my way to where I knew most of the dragon scales were. It was a section of the cave with a rough wall that looked as if Kygra used to scratch herself against. The only thing I didn't like about it was that it was located just before the opening of a large tunnel that led back further into her lair. As much as I loved dragons, I was also quite terrified to meet one. Because of this, I usually rushed over, grabbed what I could, and then ran back to the mouth of the cave.

I looked over at Root, who, for some reason, thought it would be a good idea to check out the tunnel on the opposite side of the cave. Of course, the guy who constantly reprimands me on my safety would just leave me in one of the most dangerous situations I have ever been in. I continued to make my way to the pile of scales consoling myself with the thought that if I died, it would totally be his fault, and he would feel bad about it.

I started collecting the smooth purple scales from the floor of the cave. There was an excellent selection this time around, and instead of my usual grab and run, I ended up taking my time. I must have gotten so carried away with my findings that I never noticed the draft of air coming from the tunnel slowly warmed. It didn't hit me until a large gust of sulfur-smelling air rushed past as I bent down to pick up an unusually large scale.

Now, when one meets a dragon for the first time, you think it would be polite and in the interest of the person doing the meeting to not scream, but when you are suddenly face to face with a dragon, that is impossible.

I stumbled back several steps and finally just fell over. Root, who clearly heard my scream, ran towards me. Neara reached me first and started yipping at the large purple and bronze dragon emerging from the cave. I grabbed Neara and held her close to calm her and myself down, but it wasn't working.

I thought for sure that we were about to become dinner, but instead, Kygra just stared at me with her bright green eyes. I couldn't tell if she was trying to figure out the best way to barbecue me or if she was just curious. Root finally made it to my side and positioned himself between Kygra and me.

"Hello, Kygra," he said.

If this was his plan to defend ourselves from a dragon, we were as good as dead. But to my surprise, Kygra cocked her head and paused as if to listen.

"My name is Root, and we aren't here to hurt you."

She slowly bent her head down as if to get a closer look at him. I held my breath. She sniffed him, nodded her head as if to approve, and then looked at Neara and me still sitting on the cave floor behind him.

"This is Neara, my pet fox," he said, gesturing to the squirming mass of orange fur in my arms. Kygra sniffed and nodded again. "And holding the fox is Wren, who is the current gatekeeper of our realm."

Kygra's eyes suddenly went wide. She looked me up and down, and then her eyes caught my wrist where my gatekeeper stone was. She shook her head like something had landed on her and then slowly started to back away into the tunnel, growling as she went.

"Wren, I think we should go," said Root, grabbing my arm and slowly lifting me up. We started to back up, and Kygra noticed. She stopped and then took a step forward, still growling. The only thing I remember next was sprinting with all my might out of the cave.

We threw ourselves behind the original boulder we were hiding behind and quickly checked to see if Kygra had followed us. She had disappeared.

"Well, that went well," said Root, brushing himself off.

I could strangle him right now, but I refrained. Instead, I yelled at him.

"What on earth were you doing at the other end of the cave that was so important? I almost DIED!"

"But did you die?" He sarcastically responded.

I punched him in the shoulder.

"Ow! Fine, I was looking at this." He held up a piece of paper with something written on it. I tried grabbing it out of his hand, but he jerked it away. "Uh uh, you have to ask nicely."

I rolled my eyes. "Please," I said unenthusiastically.

"That's better," He said, handing it to me.

It looked like writing, but none of it made sense.

"What strange symbols," I said. "Where could this have come from? Do you think she ate someone, and this is all that's left?"

Root took it from my hand and looked at it. "No," he

said, "I don't think so. I don't know of anyone else that comes to this island, and there haven't been any other signs of that. I have also never seen this kind of writing in my life." He folded it up and stuck it back in his pocket. "I bet Falveron would know. He has actually met Kygra before."

I was shocked. "Really?"

"Yup. It was actually your father that took him to visit her back in the day. I have heard him recount the story many times."

"My father?" I choked out.

"Yes," said Root matter of factly. "Falveron said your father always had an interest in dragons, and when Kygra showed up in the realm, he took Falveron to see her. But then your father left and locked the gate, and Kygra went into hiding and didn't want to be seen. At any rate, Falveron would probably be the only one who knows what's on this paper, seeing as no one else in the realm really knows much about dragons."

"Sorry, Wren," said Falveron after we made it back to the castle. "I have never seen anything else like this myself. That is interesting Kygra showed herself to you both, though. Hopefully, this isn't something we should be concerned about on top of everything else that is going on." He scratched his head.

"Falveron? How did my father know Kygra had shown up in the realm? Did he discover her?"

"That is a good question," said Falveron. "That was so long ago. I do remember him coming to me saying he had something to show me, and before I knew it, I was meeting Kygra face to face. It was only two days later your father left and then I had more pressing matters to attend to, so I never really thought much about it afterward. Although I did, however, go back one time to see if I could find her, but she must have been hiding in the back of her cave." I nodded, bummed that Flaveron didn't have more information for me.

By this time, I noticed it was getting late, and the sun was about to set, time for me to head back to the real world. I had my job I needed to get back to. I turned to tell Root because he always escorted me back.

"Ready?" he said before I could even ask.

"Oh. Yes," I said, his attentiveness catching me off guard. "I just need to stop at the apothecary shop on the way out if that's ok."

"Anything for you milady," said Root, bowing.

Little did Root, or anyone else for that matter, know that the new little apothecary was actually my very own shop that I secretly had someone else run for me. I kept it a secret because I wanted its success to be my own and not just because of my gatekeeper status. The idea for it actually came from the potion shelves in my mind that I used to perform magic. Then one day after some experimenting, I found that adding fairy wing dust with other elements in my realm made for perfect potions, which allowed me to turn my dream into a reality.

─────※─────

We made our way through the streets of Luma and finally came to my little shop. There was an alley on one side and another larger shop on the other. The sign over my shop's door read "Wing and Feather Apothecary".

The little bell over the door rang as I entered. My shopkeeper's head popped up behind the counter. She was a few years younger than me, short, and had dark brown hair in a messy bun on the top of her head.

"Oh, Wren!" She exclaimed, "I am so glad you are here. I had a question about th-"

I immediately hushed her and jabbed my finger at Root, who came in behind me.

Her eyes widened. "Oh, I am sorry," She stuttered. "I mean, uh, how can I help you today, Gatekeeper Wren?"

I made my way to the counter. "Hello Milly, I would like five starlight potions, please."

"Yes, of course, coming right away," she said as she disappeared into the back room.

"I heard you have a new potion in the works as well. Do you mind if I come back and take a look?" I yelled back to her.

"Oh yes, come back and see!"

I glanced back at Root, who seemed to be preoccupied with several herbs drying on the wall. I made my way around the counter and into the back room with Milly.

"Whew, that was a close one," I whispered as soon as I entered.

"Wren, I am so sorry. I didn't know Root was with you,"

"Don't worry about it!" I said, trying to calm Milly. "He didn't seem to suspect anything. He was busy looking around, which, by the way, the shop looks amazing, you are doing a great job Milly!"

She blushed and smiled. "Thank you! I do my best. I really do love this job. I am so glad you asked me to run your shop for you."

"I am glad I asked you too." I smiled back. "How have sales been?"

"Fantastic!" said Milly gesturing to the mostly empty shelves in the back. "The starlight potion is still the most popular. The fact that people now can have an unending source of light has been very helpful. Many people buy multiples so they can light every room in their homes. Word about them has spread like wildfire."

"Excellent," I said. "That is great to hear!"

"Wren! Where are you?" Root's footsteps could be heard coming towards us.

"In the back!" I yelled. "I'll be out in a minute!" I turned and leaned close to Milly. "Alright, I have to go," I whispered as

I started grabbing starlight potions from one of the shelves and shoving them in my satchel. "Thank you again for keeping this all a secret. Oh, and what was the question you had for me?"

"Oh, I was just wondering when you wanted to introduce the new potion, but that can wait for another time," she said, motioning to my messy desk strewn with fairy wing dust, different herbs for a healing potion I was working on, bottles, and notes. There were also invisible crystals, but of course, you couldn't see those. I had discovered one when I was walking through the streets of Luma one day and then suddenly tripped over what seemed like nothing. I started to feel around where I tripped because I thought for sure my foot had hit something. Sure enough, I found an invisible crystal. I pried it up and brought it back to the shop, where I halted my healing potion research, which was not going very well anyway, and started testing potions with the crystal. I found that by grinding them up and then adding the right amount of fairy wing dust, the new potion could make you temporarily invisible. After discovering this, I would spend hours watching people walk the streets in Luma, waiting for them to trip over what seemed like nothing. When they did, I would run up to where it happened and almost always find a crystal.

"Let's wait a little bit longer before we introduce this potion," I said. "I need to harvest a few more crystals so I can make a big enough batch for our release." Milly nodded and walked me back to the front counter.

"Very interesting," I said, striking up a fake conversation for Root to hear. "I can't wait for the new potion to be released. Please let me know as soon as it does."

"Yes, I will, Gatekeeper Wren," she said. "Thank you for visiting again, and have a nice day."

"That place is amazing," said Root as we left the shop. "Milly is an absolute genius."

I smiled. "Yes, yes she is."

⁂

After that, Root walked me to my gate, and I drove back home to my little apartment in the real world. My little town was dull, but it seemed even more so after I would come back from my realm. There was nothing magical about the corner gas station I passed or the cookie-cutter houses that lined the streets with their brown lawns and bare trees.

I pulled up to my apartment, which wasn't anything special either. I entered my typical white-walled, one-bedroom apartment and hung up my keys. The only thing that made it somewhat bearable was the fact I had decorated it with various things I had collected from my realm over the past year. I made my way to my living room where my workstation was and unloaded my satchel. I carefully added my dragon scales and potions to the mass of other odd trinkets and treasures on my desk. I then sat at my computer and checked for any incoming orders.

Not only did I run a secret shop in my realm, but I also ran a secret online shop in the real world. Since I was now visiting my realm so often, I needed to find a job that allowed me to go there on a regular basis. The solution I came up with was starting my own business selling items from all the realms online. The dragon scales and potions were very popular, and I badly needed to restock them. I was worried that Root would eventually find out what I was doing, but for now, he just thought I had a weird obsession with dragon scales and the small new apothecary shop. He would probably lose it if he ever found out that I was basically telling the real world I traveled to different realms, collected items from them, and sold them. But no worries, I never told anyone where the gate circle existed, and I also kept my identity a secret, so it didn't seem like a big deal to me. It was actually going so well that it was now my full-time job.

The only person that knew so far was Via, but that was because she was my best friend and because her realm, the steampunk realm, had really popular items. I was constantly asking her for more so I eventually had to tell her, but I knew she would be fine with it. As for the other gatekeepers, it was hard at first to ask them for items from their realm without being suspicious. I would just blame it on my love for all things magical and that it was a hobby to collect them, which so far seemed to be working... except, of course, for Grayson. He never let anyone in his realm. I had asked a few times, but I received a firm no every time.

I suddenly remembered that I needed to text Grayson about coming to my realm so I grabbed my cell phone and searched for his number. It felt so weird texting him. He barely had said anything to me this past year, and now here I was texting him. After conquering some last-minute doubts, I finally settled on, "Hey, I got the green light on you coming to my realm. Would next Saturday at 8 a.m. work for you?"

Chapter
~ 5 ~

It wasn't until the next day that Grayson responded with a thumbs-up emoji. Should have expected that. His communication was always the bare minimum. The rest of the week seemed to drag on. The more I thought about it, the more I just wanted it to be over with.

The day finally came, and I made my way to the gate circle. Grayson was already there when I arrived, leaning against his gate, hands in his pocket like normal. He looked up at me, and I suddenly became nervous.

"Hey, Grayson," I said, sounding like a boy going through puberty.

"Hey," he responded as he pushed himself off of his gate. "Ready to go?"

I made my way to my gate and fumbled to open it.

Grayson pulled out his gatekeeper's stone and patiently stood there waiting for me. I finally got it opened and stepped through, and to my great relief, Root was right there waiting for us as we'd planned. I was so relieved I forgot to move, and Grayson ran into my back when he came through after me.

"Sorry," I said, blushing, and quickly stepped aside.

Root could tell that I was acting funny and gave me a confused look and mouthed, "Are you ok?"

I gave him a thumbs up to reassure him through my burning cheeks. Root didn't look satisfied with my answer, but he nodded and turned to Grayson. It was then we realized that Grayson was an elf. I had thought that Grayson would stay a human like I did when I entered my realm. But looking at Grayson now it made perfect sense why he was an elf. His looks were similar to the elves at Misthold, even without the transformation. The only thing that really changed was his now pointy ears. He must have realized this as well by the way we were looking at him, and he slowly lifted his hands to feel his ears.

After a moment of silence, I realized I should probably be polite and introduce them. "Umm, Grayson, this is Root, my personal bodyguard. And Root, this is Grayson."

Root stuck out his hand. Grayson looked at it for a moment and then shook it. It was a very firm handshake.

"Shall we get going?" I asked.

"Yes, sounds good," said Root, finally letting go of

Grayson's hand.

We made our way down into Luma. I tried to make conversation to ease all the weird tension going on by pointing out the sights to Grayson. At one point Grayson asked about the powers of our realm. Since he had a gatekeeper stone, it meant that he could not only carry his own powers into the realm but also wield the powers of our realm. I showed him a few of my favorite tricks, and he could replicate them all on the first try. Grayson's magic skills were very impressive, and I noticed Root following just a little closer behind us.

We soon arrived in the dining hall having lunch with Flaveron and his family.

"So Grayson, what do you think of our realm so far," said Falveron, trying to strike up a conversation with Grayson for the 5th time.

"It's great," said Grayson, who once again killed the conversation instantaneously and continued eating. He at least seemed to like the food.

The clinking of the utensils on the plates continued to be the only noise.

"Did you figure out anything for the dwarves yet?" I finally asked Falveron. I couldn't take the awkward silence.

"I have some ideas," said Falveron, wiping his mouth and putting down his fork. "That was something I wanted to talk to you about after your trip with Root."

"What trip?" said Grayson.

"We are taking a trip to see the stoneless village down south. Wren and I have been planning this for a while now because she hasn't been there yet," said Root.

"Stoneless?"

"Yes, it means they don't have any working gate key gemstones. So no magic."

"Got it," said Grayson

"Is that still ok, Falveron?" I said, "If we need to stay and work on what needs to be done about the dwarves, I am definitely willing to stay."

"Oh, no, no, you go," said Falveron. "We still have five more days till Dorgan comes back. You and Root go have fun. I can hold things down here. Besides, I would like an update on how the village is doing. It's been a while since our last visit."

"Can I go?" asked Grayson. Everyone stopped eating and looked at him.

"Well, this was a trip Wren and I had planned and-" Root began.

"Yes, you can come." I found myself blurting out. Root glared at me. "Umm, it is a two-night trip, just to let you know."

"I've got nothing better to do," said Grayson, leaning back in his chair. Root did not look amused.

"Great," I said, "Shall we get ready, then?"

Root rolled his eyes and stood up. "I'll get the horses ready. Would you like to come with me to help?" he asked, turning to Grayson.

"Sure," said Grayson, glancing at me.

"You two have fun." I said, "I'll get our packs ready."

They left the room, and I stood up to leave.

"What an interesting person, this Grayson," said Falveron. "I can't quite understand him."

"Welcome to my life," I said.

"Are you sure it's a good idea to bring him on this trip?"

My heart sank. "I think it will be ok. And besides, I have Root."

"That is true," sighed Falveron. "Just be safe."

༺❀༻

We got ready and headed out. Root decided to take the scenic route down to the stoneless village, stopping at a few landmarks. The first of these was the wishing well, which we reached within the hour. It was said that if you threw in a coin and made a wish, it would come true. The larger the amount of the coin, the more likely it would come true. Root pulled out a thick gold coin and gave it to me when we arrived. After thinking about it for a little bit, I made a wish and threw it in. When it hit the bottom, the sound it made wasn't a splash but more like the twinkle of wind chimes that echoed for what seemed like a whole minute. Next, Root pulled out a silver coin, made a wish, and threw it in, the well making the same twinkling noise.

"You want to make a wish?" I asked Grayson.

He shrugged his shoulders and pulled out a quarter from the real world and nonchalantly threw it in. When it hit the bottom though, it sounded more like a small chipmunk drowning. I don't think the well liked his quarter.

⁂

Next, we came to Laqumirth. It was the only place on the island that was absolutely disgusting. It was a large bubbling pool of mud that smelled like rotten pumpkins, dead fish, and a dirty diaper all at once. All the trees around the swamp were blackened and shriveled. Root said the spot had been slowly growing over the years. He took notes on it's size to report back to Falveron. I asked Root why it was there, and he had no idea. Grayson looked intrigued by it but didn't say anything.

We continued on, and to my surprise, Grayson seemed to actually be enjoying himself. He even started whistling what I thought sounded like the opening sound to that old Robin Hood movie at one point. But even though his spirits seemed to be lifted, he still didn't say much.

⁂

We finally reached the stoneless village just as the sun

was setting. The elder of the village, a large burly man, named Benson, came out to greet us.

"Welcome to Elyra!" bellowed Benson cheerfully. "Root! Good to see you again. It's been a while."

Root winced under the slap that Benson gave him on the back. "Good to see you too, Benson," he rubbed his shoulder but still smiled.

"Who are your friends here?"

"This is Wren, the gatekeeper of our realm," said Root, bringing me forward.

"The gatekeeper!" Bellowed Benson. "What a pleasure to finally meet you." He shook my hand so hard I thought my arm was going to come off.

"And this is Grayson," continued Root. "He is also a gatekeeper but to realm number six."

"Must be a depressing realm," said Benson laughing. "You look as if the most exciting thing you've ever done in your life is breathe. No worries, we'll fix that. Nothing like a day in Elyra to cure you of, well, depression." Benson laughed louder and slapped Grayson on the back.

Grayson was not amused.

"Well, you must have had a long day, and it's getting late," said Benson, leading the way through the village. "Let's get you to the guest houses, and we will get you all settled in. Then tomorrow, I can show you around."

"You glad you came on this trip?" I laughed, nudging

Grayson.

"Oh ya, totally, so fun," replied Grayson sarcastically. Regardless, I was able to catch him smiling before he turned away.

<hr />

The next day was amazing. Benson introduced us to his family and showed us around the village. Children ran out of houses to greet us and everyone was so friendly. Benson told everyone we were having a feast in our honor later that night. The excitement that filled the village from this news was contagious. Everyone went to work preparing for the night.

We went back to Benson's house and helped his family make pastries. Root stood off to the side and just watched us. Guess he didn't like baking. Grayson, to my surprise, offered to help. He got so into it that at one point, I heard him laugh as one of Benson's kids accidentally dumped flour all over the table and floor. The kids started throwing the unusable flour at each other, and even Grayson picked some up and dumped it in my hair, still laughing. I retaliated and shoved flour in his face.

<hr />

Night finally came, and we made our way to a large clearing with the longest table I'd ever seen. The table was already full of the delicious food the villagers had been preparing all day. Lanterns filled the trees that surrounded the clearing, and music drifted through the air. For a village that didn't have any magic, it was one of the most magical things I had ever seen.

After eating my fill of some of the most delicious food I had ever tasted and dancing with so many villagers I lost count, I decided to take a break. I had noticed that I heard a waterfall in the distance earlier and decided to go check it out. I thought about telling Root just in case, but he had been a party pooper all night. He was in a weird mood, skulking about, not engaging in anything or with anyone but intently watching me. However, he was stuck in a long-winded conversation with Benson that he clearly did not want to be a part of, so I took this as my opportunity to slip away on my own.

I took a path that seemed to be headed towards the sound of the rushing water, and soon falls came into view, glittering in the moonlight. I closed my eyes and felt the mist brush my face.

"Pretty amazing, huh?" came a voice directly behind me. I jumped and almost fell over, but I impressively kept myself from screaming.

"Gosh, Grayson," I said angrily, "I almost died of a heart attack. Next time give me a little warning, will ya?"

He laughed, which immediately made my anger dissipate.

"What are you doing here anyway?" I asked as I looked for a place to sit.

"I saw you leave and was wondering what you were up to," he said, following me. "I was also curious about the waterfall." He added.

"Right," I said as I sat down on a large boulder overlooking the waterfall.

"Where's your bodyguard?" Grayson sat down next to me.

"Umm, back at the party, I think," I replied.

Grayson grunted and nodded. "So what do you think?" he leaned back on his elbows.

"Of what?"

"Of Elyra," he said. "It's pretty crazy how happy they are for a village without any magic."

I took a moment to ponder this. "You are right. It's been a while since I've had this much fun. Especially baking pastries with the kids."

"Ya, you look pretty great with white hair, just saying." Said Grayson chuckling. "You will age well."

I punched his arm.

"Ow, what was that for! I complimented you!" he said.

I awkwardly laughed it off.

"What about you? What do you think?" I asked.

"I think," he said, pausing for effect, "That Root snores louder than a jet taking off." His comment caught me off guard, and I burst out laughing, which caused him to start laughing too.

"Wren," said Grayson after a minute.

"Uhh, yes?" I said, impressed with how much he was talking for once.

"Which do you prefer? This realm or the real world?"

I scrunched my face, for some reason feeling offended by the question. I took a deep breath to compose myself.

"To be honest, it's a question I guess I think about often," I finally said. I paused, but Grayson remained silent, waiting for me to continue. "One day, several months ago, I woke up one morning and made up my mind to go live in my realm full time. I packed up a few necessities and just left. Halfway to the gate circle, it suddenly hit me that I hadn't even said goodbye to anyone. I wanted so badly to just leave the real world and live in my realm that the people I loved didn't even cross my mind. Not to mention I had also left most of my stuff in an apartment that I hadn't even canceled my rent on. I was just leaving a mess for everyone else to deal with. It scared me because that is not who I was or who I wanted to be as a person. I ran back to my apartment, immediately unpacked my bag, and vowed that I would do my best to be present in the real world. Not going to lie though, it's still something I struggle with. I visit my realm often and can always feel the pull of it."

I looked over at Grayson, who was staring at me intently.

"Wow, sorry," I said, suddenly feeling awkward. "I have never really told anyone that before. I know it sounds bad, but

I really do love my parents and the friends I have in the real world."

"I don't doubt that at all. You are one of the kindest, most caring people I know."

What an odd thing for him to say. It's not like he even knew me that well.

"So uh, do your parents know that you come here?" He asked, suddenly sitting up.

"No," I said, cringing at the thought of what I was going to explain next. "I technically stole the gatekeeper's stone from my father. I found it in my parent's closet when I was helping them move last year. It was tucked away in a leather pouch that also contained a map of our town on a tattered piece of paper that led me to the gate circle. The rest is history. There have been moments where I have wanted to tell my dad that I found it," I sighed at the thought, "but at the same time, I have been scared my dad will demand it back and take this all away from me. So for now I don't say anything and he has never mentioned it."

"Do you still talk to your dad regularly?"

"Of course," I said. "My parents are always checking in on me. I just don't see them in person as much anymore since they moved to the big city."

Grayson nodded.

"Anyway, what about you? How did you get your gatekeeper's stone?"

"Well, just like your family, my stone was passed down from generation to generation. My mom was the previous gatekeeper of my realm. But she passed away several years ago..." He trailed off and just sat there quietly.

"I'm sorry," I said, not wanting to pry any further. I could tell it wasn't a subject he really wanted to talk about.

"So what exactly is your realm?" I could tell I was pushing my luck, but maybe he would find this a welcoming subject change. I could immediately tell that it was bad timing on my part.

"Wren, I don't really-"

"Wren!" interrupted Root's voice in the distance.

Grayson groaned and stood up. Before I could jump up too, Root appeared below the boulder we were sitting on.

"There you are," said Root. "I have been looking for you everywhere." He looked over at Grayson, who was still standing there. Neither of us said anything.

"Is everything ok, Wren?" He asked.

"Oh, uh, yes!" I said, finally standing to my feet. "We were just chatting." I made my way to the edge of the rock in an attempt to get down. Grayson rushed up to me to help me down, and Root did the same.

"It's fine. I got you," said Root, holding out his hand. I looked back at Grayson, who also had his hand out, but he quickly took it back.

"Thank you," I said, letting Root help me down. Grayson

jumped down beside us and entered a brief staring contest with Root.

"Well, it's getting late, and I am going to turn in," said Grayson, breaking their intense eye contact. He abruptly turned and started making his way down the path back to the village. "Nice talking to you, Wren."

"You too!" I said, waving after him.

"Wren," said Root when Grayson had left.

"What?" I sighed, turning towards him in frustration.

"You really need to be careful! Why did you leave me behind!"

"I just needed to get away for a bit. I feel like you are always breathing down my neck. You have also been a stick in the mud, and I don't find it fun to be around you when you are like that."

"Wren!" said Root. "You are the one who asked me to protect you, and I take this job very seriously. I still have my concerns about Grayson and I want you to be safe."

"I know!" I said, realizing that my attitude could use some adjusting. "I'm sorry. it's just that I was so close to figuring out what Grayson's realm was, and you kind of ruined the moment."

Root let out a frustrated sigh. "Alright, well, at least let me know where you are going next time, ok?"

"Fine," I said. "As long as you promise to lighten up. I am starting to think that Grayson is not so bad after all, so you don't need to worry as much."

"That's what concerns me," mumbled Root.

I glared at him.

"Ugg, fine," he said, "I'll promise to lighten up."

"Much better," I said.

We spent the night and then packed up early the following day to head back. Grayson made me laugh again when I asked him how he slept, and all he did was plug his ears and point at Root.

Even though Root promised to lighten up, he didn't seem much different. He also seemed to be in a hurry to get back to the castle, and we galloped most of the way back. We made it back to the castle courtyard in record time. But before I could even dismount my horse, a porter came running out of the castle towards us. "Gatekeeper Wren," he said, clearly panicking. "The dwarf king has returned a few days early and is demanding more gemstones. Lord Falveron would like to see you this instant!"

Chapter
6

I took off running towards the castle with Root and Grayson.

We heard the dwarf king before we saw him. He was in the great hall with Falveron. Several guards stood outside the door, and even more were inside.

"But I am demanding them now!" said the dwarf king, slamming his fist on the meeting table.

"King Dorgan, please, you arrived three days early. We aren't quite ready with a response yet," Falveron paused as he saw us enter. "Ah Wren, I am glad you are here," He said calmly, gesturing to the three empty chairs to his right. Grayson looked as if he was going to leave, but I motioned for him to sit down. It was probably good for him to see this.

"Who is this?" Bellowed the king as Grayson sat down.

"This is Gatekeeper Grayson of realm six," I responded.

The king stared at him for a moment.

"Well, I don't care. I am here for my gemstones, which," He said, glaring at me, "seemed to have not been collected."

Falveron stepped in. "Please don't look to Wren for answers. The issue lies with me. I planned to discuss your current issue with Wren when she returned from their trip. I am afraid you have caught us off guard."

"This is something you should have been discussing days ago!" the dwarf king roared. "I can see now how poorly this realm is run. If I ran this realm, we would be a thousand times better off. In fact, that gives me an idea..." He started reaching for the handle of his ax.

"I would like to say something," came Grayson's voice from behind me.

Astonished, I turned around to look at him.

"I understand you have a shortage of working gate key gemstones, is that correct?" continued Grayson.

"Yes," said Dorgan angrily.

"Might I suggest checking other realms for working gemstones?"

We all sat there blinking.

"Well, you see, when the power was taken from the gemstones years ago, there was a war between the realms. The reason for this was because many people had collected the twelve different gemstones so they could visit any realm they wanted, whenever they wanted. But when the power was taken from the gemstones, many people started fighting over the remaining working gemstones. It got so bad that realms started locking their gates and banning anyone from leaving or entering. The space realm was the only one that didn't get involved and just locked their gate immediately. I would bet that there are still many working gemstones for all the realms just lying around in there. If you would like, I could talk to Launch, the space realms gatekeeper, to see if he could look around for me."

There was silence for a moment, all of us processing what we had just heard.

"How soon can you make this happen?" Asked the dwarf king skeptically.

"Well, I am just about to leave this realm. I could contact him immediately. We may need to give him a day or so to go check, but I think we could potentially have them for you by the day you said you'd originally return."

The dwarf king scratched his beard for a moment. He looked at his attendant, who nodded. "Fine," He said, standing up. "Three days it is." He abruptly left without saying goodbye.

The hall was suddenly quiet.

"I'm a genius," said Grayson, sitting back in his chair.

"Is what you said true?" asked Root.

"Of course," said Grayson.

"Why didn't you tell me this before?" I asked, exasperated.

"You never asked," He responded. I glared at him. "Also, I forgot about that till now. I know most of the realms were able to trade over the years, and every realm now seems to have all its own gemstones, but I remembered my mother telling me that the space realm was the only one that didn't participate in all that. I really think they could have quite a few in there. I will just send him a message, and we can meet him when we leave the realm."

I could have jumped up and hugged him.

"Well," exclaimed Falveron, "That is a way better plan than what I had. I wish you the best of luck and thank you for your assistance. I was very worried about the way things were heading."

We got ready to leave. As we walked back up to the gate, Grayson messaged Launch. Root came with us, of course, although he seemed slightly more relaxed.

We said goodbye to Root as we reached the gate. I opened it up, and Grayson went through it first.

"Alright, he seems ok." said Root as soon as Grayson disappeared through the gate. "Especially if he can pull this off."

"See! I told you." I smiled. Root rolled his eyes.

I said goodbye and stepped through the gate. I bumped into Grayson's back, and before I could ask anything, he signaled for me to be quiet.

"What's wrong?" I whispered in his ear.

"Gate eleven is open," He said, concerned. I peered around his shoulder and saw the gate, the light purplish color of the circular glass in its keystone was glowing, and its open portal was swirling with the same misty color. Grayson slowly made his way towards the gate, looking in all directions. I stayed by my gate, the sound of my open portal humming behind me. Gate two suddenly sprang to life, and Launch jumped out, which startled Grayson. At the exact same time, I felt someone grab me from behind and start to pull me off of the gate circle. I barely got out a scream before I felt a large hand cover my mouth.

Chapter 7

Whoever was holding me was insanely strong. He was able to keep me from escaping with just one hand covering my mouth and pressing me against his chest. I suddenly felt something cold press up against the back of my neck. Was it a gun? I panicked even more but then remembered Root's training. I entered the potion shelves in my mind and grabbed the one labeled fireball. I drank it, but instead of forming a fireball, my entire body felt as if it was trying to rip itself in half, and the cool feeling from the object pressed on the back of my neck was replaced with a blazing heat. I tried to scream, but the feeling was so intense that no words came out and my vision began to fade.

"Wren!" I heard Grayson yell and turned my head just enough to catch his blurry image running towards me, his hand waving through the air. I suddenly heard my captor gasp and take a step back. He must have tripped over something because I fell from his grasp, but before I hit the ground, Grayson caught my hand and stopped me. I slumped against his chest, finding that I could no longer stand. He gently guided me to the ground. My attacker was now in front of us, sprawled out on the ground behind a boulder that Grayson must have conjured for him to trip over. For a second, I was confused because the man who was lying there was a spindly little fellow wearing a long dark blue robe and a funny-looking hat. He looked like a prepubescent merlin. Even though I was on the verge of passing out, I still blushed at the thought that this tiny wafer of a wizard was able to overtake me. He stood back up and made his way towards us. He was bleeding from his forehead, and he wiped it away with the back of his hand, which contained a small black object.

Launch skidded in between the wizard and us. As he did, he grabbed some sort of device at his hip, slammed his gatekeeper's stone into the bottom of it, causing light to extend from the other end into a sword.

"I don't have time for this!" yelled the wizard. He lifted his hand up, and the vines that were wrapped around gate twelve behind us sprung to life. They shot past us, wrapped themselves around Launch, and started dragging him back towards the gate.

Grayson, who was still on the ground with me, shifted

himself to be in between the wizard and me. A dark cloud materialized above our heads, and a loud clap of thunder echoed between the gates.

"It's going to be ok," he whispered to me, his serious face going in and out of view. He slowly stood up, his hands outstretched on either side of him. The wizard backed up nervously. Launch, who must have made quick work of the vines with his sword, appeared next to Grayson.

"I got this," growled Grayson. "You get Wren out of here."

The air crackled with electricity, and I could feel the hair on my arm start to stand on end as Launch came to my side. He quickly scooped me up and made his way back to his gate. I thought we would jump through it, but he stopped just outside of it. A bright flash of light filled the sky, and a loud explosion followed. Launch bent over to shield me until the blast subsided. We turned around just in time to see the little wizard jump back through gate eleven, followed by Grayson.

"No!" yelled Launch as he dashed towards the gate with me still in his arms. Before he could reach it, the gate snapped shut, the giant cloud above us vanished and we were left in the silence of the forest.

Between losing Grayson to gate eleven and the pain in the back of my neck, I could feel myself losing consciousness. The last thing I remember before completely blacking out was Launch saying something about going to get

Grayson. He slipped through his own gate and I slipped into unconsciousness.

※

When I finally awoke, I found myself in Via's clock tower apartment, which meant I was in the Steampunk realm. The sunlight was streaming in through the giant clock faces on each side of the large room, and I could hear people bustling about in the streets below. I was lying in the little cot that she slept in at the back corner of the room. I could see her little kitchen in the opposite corner, dishes piled high in the sink, as usual. Several desks and workstations were randomly situated around the room as well, and all contained a mess of papers, little trinkets, and tools. In the back of the room was a hole in the floor that opened up to the spiral staircase from which I could now hear footsteps. I sat up to get a better view of the opening, but my movement sent a sharp pain shooting through the back of my neck. I let out a yelp. Via's head appeared at the top of the stairway.

"You're awake!" She yelled, running up to me. She wrapped me in a big hug.

I winced again.

"Sorry!" she said, taking a step back. "Trez said you would be pretty sore after what you experienced, especially the base of your neck. By the way, I need to change your bandage." She jumped over to a small table where gauzes, tapes, and bandages were piled high, along with a small bottle containing some sort of white salve.

"What exactly happened to my neck?" I asked, reaching back to feel what was wrong.

"Don't touch it!" said Via, rushing back. "You got burned pretty badly. Trez said he did the best he could for it but it would still leave a permanent mark. At least it looks pretty awesome. You want to see it?"

I nodded.

She carefully brought me over to her small vanity at one end of the room and handed me a mirror. I watched as she unbandaged the back of my neck.

"How long was I out for?"

"Well, Trez brought you here last night, so almost 24 hours. He told me you would be out for a while. Your injury was pretty extensive."

"Ya, I remember seeing him before I totally blacked out," I said. "Via! What happened to Grayson? And Launch? I saw Grayson run into gate eleven, and then Launch said he was going to go get him and disappeared into his own gate!"

"It's ok, Wren!" said Via, patting my shoulder. I winced again. "Trez told me I was to keep you calm and that getting worked up won't help. He came to check on you this morning and said that Grayson and Launch are both ok. I don't know the details, though."

I calmed down, letting all this information sink in.

"You ready to look?"

I held up the mirror she gave me so I could see it through the reflection in the vanity mirror. I gasped. The burn mark was an odd shape, bright red, and oozing slightly. Even though it didn't look great, it already seemed to be healing.

"This definitely has something to do with magic," said Via. "Do you know what it was that they put on your back?"

"No," I sighed. "I was kind of preoccupied with just trying not to die, although I do vaguely remember him holding something dark and small in his hand after Grayson pulled me from his grasp."

"Interesting," said Via. "Well, whatever the object was, it was definitely some kind of circular shape because the burn mark it made is a jagged half circle. The reason it is only a half circle is because there is a clear line down your back that it never crossed."

I took a closer look at the little mirror and confirmed what Via had said. "I guess it kind of makes sense. I did feel like my body was trying to split in half. It was a terrifying feeling, especially in my chest."

Via looked concerned. "Well, I am glad you are here in one piece... literally." She laughed at her own pun, realized I wasn't laughing, and then continued. "I was so worried when Trez sent the message that you were hurt and wanted the gate opened so he could get you in here to safety. Good thing I live right above our gate. He carried you up here and then left immediately to check on Grayson and Launch." She reached for the bottle with the salve in it and popped off the cork.

"What is that? I asked as she scraped out the remainder of its contents and spread it over my wound.

"Something Trez gave me this morning," she said. "It has helped tremendously, your burn looked way worse before. Good thing he had this little bit left."

Via slapped a new bandage on, causing me to wince once again. She glanced over at the small cane she kept her gatekeeper stone on. It was glowing a deep red for a moment and then changed to its normal color. She jumped up, grabbed the cane, and went over to the fireman's pole she used to get down to the main floor of the clock tower. "Well, Grayson just asked me if he and Launch could come in. Told you they were alright. Be right back!" She disappeared down the hole.

My heart skipped a beat, and I hurriedly tried to fix my hair in the vanity mirror. I was a mess. I gave up just as Grayson, Launch, and Via appeared at the top of the steps. Grayson looked completely fine, but I did notice that Launch had a large bruise on his head.

"I am glad to see you're awake," Grayson said. "I am so sorry I left you, but I wanted to make sure that whoever that guy was who attacked you never messed with you again. I am so glad that Launch was able to get Trez to help you, though." He came up and stood in front of me while Launch still stood at the top of the stairs taking in Via's apartment.

"Oh, it's totally fine," I replied. "Other than feeling tired and this burn on my back, I am doing great."

"Is it bad?" he asked. "Trez was telling me about it. Do you mind if I see it?"

"Umm, sure, Via just bandaged it, but I am sure she won't mind if you take a look at it." I turned around, and Grayson suddenly let out a laugh.

"What?" I asked.

"Well, Via's method of bandaging is umm, well, horrible," he said, whispering the last word so Via couldn't hear. Launch had asked her about something on her workstation, and she was currently busy showing it to him.

I laughed. "Well she isn't what I would describe as gentle, that's for sure."

Grayson proceeded to gently take off the bandage. Silence followed.

"Grayson? What's wrong? Does it look ok?"

He paused a second and then started bandaging it up again. "Yes, sorry, everything is fine. It looks pretty good actually. Trez did a great job with it." I caught a glimpse of his face in the vanity mirror. A look of concern and deep thought was etched across his face. I was too nervous to ask any further questions.

"Hey! What are you doing?" yelled Via as Grayson finished up. She came running over. "I just bandaged that!"

"Just wanted to take a look at it." said Grayson "besides,

doesn't it look much better?" The new bandage did feel a lot more secure.

She huffed and crossed her arms but didn't respond. She knew he was right.

Launch leaned over to look at the bandage.

"Did you want to see it?" I asked.

"Oh no, I'm good," said Launch, taking a step back. "I don't do great with those kinds of things," he gently touched the bruise on his head.

"So what exactly happened to you guys?" I asked.

"Ya, tell us the whole story," said Via, settling down in a chair beside my bed. I was enjoying how comfortable this felt, Grayson being open, Launch, and Via chatting. It felt good.

"Well," said Grayson, "After the little wizard dude blocked my lightning attack, he dodged back in gate eleven, and I followed. I was greeted by the gatekeeper, who immediately closed the gate after I got in. He, uh, started fighting me, and then more of his goons showed up and joined in the fight, including the wizard. That is when Launch showed up with his rocket ship and crashed it into the gatekeeper."

"I am sorry, what?" interrupted Via.

"Shhhh, let him finish," I said, totally intrigued by this story.

"The blast caused all of the gatekeeper's sidekicks to fly back, but unfortunately, it didn't seem to affect the gatekeeper at all. When the smoke cleared, he was still standing there as if nothing happened."

"Wait, Launch, how did you survive the crash?" asked Via.

"I ejected just before impact," said Launch.

Via sat there with her mouth wide open in adoration.

"Launch and I were ready to fight him, but instead, he offered to let us go," continued Grayson. "So he opened the gate and let us go."

Launch shrugged. "Ya, that was a little odd. But we'll take it. At least we both made it out in one piece."

"Wow," whispered Via.

"So wait, Launch, how did you get into the realm?" I asked, getting excited. "I thought you were still working on it."

"I was," said Launch. "But I already had enough power to break through two realm barriers, as I said in the meeting. Up until now, I used that power to break out of my realm and then back in. I just hadn't tested it out on another realm yet. Technically, I would need to have enough power to break through four realm barriers to get back home."

"Wait, what are realm barriers?" asked Via.

"So you know how if you travel too far in one direction in your realm, you eventually end right back where you started?"

"Oh, like when we sail north in my realm, and it loops us around, and we end up on the south side of the island, right?" I said.

"Exactly," said Launch. "I figured out a way to create a field that disrupts that barrier so I can break through instead of looping back around."

"But wait," said Via, "Once you break through your realm wall, where do you go?"

"The void. You know, the place I mentioned in the meeting." None of us said anything. He sighed and continued. "As I said, it's where all of our realms are located. They are suspended in what looks like giant bubbles. From there, all I had to do was make my way to realm eleven and break through. Glad it worked out. I was nervous."

"So we now know where gate eleven's stone is," I said slowly. "We need to go back and get it! Do you have more power?"

"Well, I did crash the spaceship that got me there," said Launch. "But no worries, I have a second one that I was working on, which will be ready to go soon."

"Really?" I said.

"Yes, but the main problem is storing up enough energy in the Sun Stones that I use to power the ship. It will probably take me two months. Not to mention I would like to have enough energy to make it back out of the realm and back into mine in case we can't get the gatekeeper's stone back. So maybe four months then."

"Four months!" I said, exasperated. "But we need answers now!"

"Wren," said Grayson calmly, "I know you are concerned with things in your realm, but the other reason I came was to give you these."

He reached into his coat pocket and pulled out a small container. He pressed the top of it, and it slowly opened up to reveal a small pile of glowing light blue gemstones.

I looked up at Grayson in disbelief.

"As I said, Launch asked around, and he ended up finding some for you."

Tears began to fill my eyes. "Thank you," I whispered as I took the little box and clutched it to my chest. "This means so much." I looked up, and Grayson was staring at me.

He lifted his hand as if he was about to brush my hair back, but he stopped himself and shoved his hand back into his pocket. "That should pacify them for a while anyway," He suddenly looked away and cleared his throat. "But Launch has agreed to start charging up his sun stones immediately, and we can start exploring more. It's just going to take a little time."

Launch nodded.

"In the meantime, I am very concerned about this gate eleven and the fact it's sending out people to attack us. I decided to call another meeting to let everyone know about what happened but wanted to check in with you before I sent out a message. Would three days from now work for you all? I want to give Wren time to recover."

"Thank you," I said. "That works for me."

Via and Launch agreed too.

"Perfect," said Grayson. He took his gatekeeper's stone, and a few seconds later, our stones lit up, and I heard Grayson's voice in my head calling for the emergency meeting. As soon as it was finished playing in my mind, he stood up.

"Well, time to go. I'll see you later." He said, making his way to the stairs again.

Launch quickly stood up and followed Grayson.

Just before they disappeared down the stairs, Grayson stopped. "Oh," he said, "Please let me know if and when you would like to go home before the meeting. It's not safe with gate eleven planning who knows what."

"Oh, well, I was hoping to get back as soon as possible, maybe even tonight?"

Via glared at me. "Wren, you live by yourself, at least let me watch you one more night here, and then tomorrow morning you can go." For a fourteen-year-old, she sometimes acted like my mom.

"Fine," I responded. I was still feeling pretty weak.

"Ok, just send me a message in the morning when you want to go, and I'll come get you. I plan on hanging around here to keep an eye on things anyway," said Grayson as he headed down the stairs.

Via jumped up to follow. "Well, that was weird." She yelled up as soon as the gate was closed. She kept talking as she stomped back up. "But how fun! I had visitors to my realm!

It's rare that people come here other than you. Oh, and it turns out Launch and I have a lot in common. While you two were getting all cozy, I was showing him one of my projects, and he seemed super interested and understood everything I was saying!" She finally appeared at the top of the stairs.

"What do you mean getting cozy?" I fussed. "He was just checking on me for like two minutes. And if you hadn't noticed, he is still pretty rough around the edges."

"I don't know," smirked Via. "He also got the gemstones for you. Something is definitely going on with him. I haven't seen him this friendly in, well, forever." She winked at me.

⁂

Between Via's engineer stew and another full night's rest, I felt like my normal self by the next morning. Even my burn looked a million times better and had stopped hurting. I grabbed my things and messaged Grayson, and he met us just outside Via's gate like he said.

Before going back to my house, I asked Grayson if we could drop off the gate key gemstones he'd given me first. The sooner I got them to Falveron, the better. He agreed, and we went through my gate. I wrote a note on a piece of paper and, with my magic, sent it to Root. A few minutes later, a reply came.

"Root will meet us up here," I told Grayson. "I am not sure I am totally up for having to climb back up here if we go down."

Grayson nodded and sat down on the grass, and I joined him. It would take Root about thirty minutes to get here, so we had some time to kill. I figured it would be a good time to ask him about his realm, but since he seemed to dodge the question every time, I decided to try a new tactic.

After about five minutes of psyching myself up, I finally spoke up, "Hey, I have a question."

"I am not telling you what's in my realm," He said bluntly.

"Well, I know that, but I actually had a different question," I said.

"Ok, what is it?"

"Well, umm, so I have been collecting items from all the realms for fun, and yours is a realm I haven't gotten anything from yet."

"You can't go in my realm, Wren. I told you that!"

"I know. I don't want to go into your realm. I was just wondering if you could bring me back something from it."

He paused and stared up at the sky, thinking. "Well, what exactly would you want?"

"Oh, anything really. Just as long as it's from your realm."

He paused again. I held my breath.

"Fine," he said.

I jumped up, clapped my hands together, and squealed.

"Are you serious? Really?" I leaned over to get a closer look at his face to see if he was just kidding or not.

He sighed again and went from looking at the sky to looking at me, suddenly realizing I had scooted closer to him. He quickly backed off. "Gosh Wren, yes! But calm down, it's not going to be anything crazy."

"Oh, that's fine. I don't really care what it is," I said, beaming, mostly from excitement but partly because I made him uncomfortable.

We were quiet after that, Grayson thinking of who knows what and me internally reveling over the fact I'd gotten him to say yes.

***

Root finally showed up. He was visibly excited about the gemstones and thanked Grayson. We also relayed to him what happened and even showed him my scar.

"Wren," he said mournfully, "I didn't realize you would be in danger outside of the realm. Do you need me to come with you from now on?"

"I can help with that," Grayson said. He said it so abruptly it caught both Root and me off guard. "Well, what I mean by that is that I live in the real world, and it would be easier for me to walk her home. Besides, it would mean that you would need to keep the gatekeeping stone with you to lock it when you get back from dropping her off. Then she wouldn't have it to get back in."

"I mean, it makes sense," said Root.

"Oh, umm, yes, I would be totally fine with that." I stuttered.

"Ok, it's settled then," said Root. "You better take good care of her," he stared down Grayson.

Grayson just nodded

"Well then," said Root, "I better get going. The sooner these get to the dwarf king, the better."

We said our goodbyes, and we headed back out to the gate circle. Nothing else was really said as Grayson walked me back. My heart was still pounding, though. Was it because I was scared of Grayson? Was it because after he explained why he should be the one to walk me home, I realized he had already thoroughly thought it through. But why? I was beginning to think Via might be onto something.

Chapter
8

The next couple of days seemed so long. I had to catch up on things. I was gone a whole two days more than I had planned and work was piling up. I only had a few orders I needed to ship for my online business but what I really needed to catch up on was making videos. I was so excited about Grayson finally getting me something from his realm I decided to make a video letting everyone know that I would be showing them this mysterious item soon. Everyone seemed just as intrigued as I was.

The day finally came for our meeting. Grayson texted me, and we met at the spot we would park our cars before walking to the gate circle. He got out of his car and immediately handed me a small jar filled with what looked like tiny shiny black rocks.

"Umm, what's this?" I asked

"You said you wanted something from my realm." He said.

"Oh," I said disappointedly, "I mean, it just looks like a jar of dirt."

"You don't want it, then give it back," He said in a strange accent.

"No!" I said, pulling it away from him. He turned and ducked under the vines to the secret path. "Wait, did you just quote that pirate movie?" I yelled as I ran after him.

As we made our way to the gate circle, I kept turning the jar over in my hands, trying to figure out what the theme of his realm could possibly be. It was so like Grayson to give me a jar of shiny-looking dirt. The more I looked at it, the more it reminded me of molten lava. Maybe his realm was some sort of dark, mysterious realm.

We finally arrived at the gate circle, and Grayson made the table appear. We arrived early, so no one was there yet. We sat in silence for a moment, waiting for the others to show when suddenly I heard someone crying coming from the woods just behind gate three. Isla appeared through the thick trees and stumbled onto the gate circle, her clothes looked disheveled, and her dirty hands covered her face.

"Isla?" I said softly.

She jerked her head up and saw Grayson and me sitting at the table.

"Wren!" She gasped, running up to me and throwing herself into me. She started rambling. "I thought our meeting was yesterday for some reason, so I came, and I sat here forever, but no one showed up, but then someone jumped me from behind and took my gatekeeper's stone, and they are probably destroying my realm as we speak and my family is going to blame me for it all, and I haven't been able to contact anyone because I don't have the stone and my family is going to kill me..." her rambling turned into sobbing.

Just then, Trez, Jumana, and Via appeared from their gates.

"What's going on?" Asked Trez.

"Sounds like Isla's gatekeeper's stone was stolen," I said, still patting her back and trying to comfort her.

"Trez, you can help me!" Isla burst out. "They took it and went into my realm, but you can get me there, right?"

Trez suddenly looked nervous. "Well, technically, yes, I can."

"Wait, what?" I said.

Isla turned back to me, getting more and more excited.

"You don't know?" She asked.

"Don't know what?" Via and I said simultaneously.

"The mermaid realm and the pirate realm are

connected."

Via and I stood there with our mouths open. I looked around at Grayson and Jumana, who already seemed to have known this.

"Umm, why wasn't this ever mentioned before?" I asked Trez.

"Well, you never asked." He said, clearly not wanting to talk about the subject any further.

"Trez even used to-" began Isla.

Trez cut her off by loudly clearing his throat.

Grayson spoke up next. "Isla, what did this person look like?"

"Well, it was a girl, and she had short dark hair. She moved so fast I couldn't tell you any defining features, though."

Grayson looked concerned. "Well, it seems like there's more than just one person trying to mess with us." He looked at me.

Just then, Launch and Fynne appeared through their own gates. Launch took in the scene, and Fynne immediately came up to us. "Wren, are you ok? What's wrong with Isla?"

Before I could answer, Trez spoke up. "Since we are all here, let's just go ahead and start the meeting so we can explain what's going on to everyone. I want to hear about what happened to Wren as well."

We all sat down. For some reason, I suddenly felt vulnerable. Two attacks already happened at the gate circle, and here we were, like sitting ducks around our table. I looked towards Grayson, who seemed to be thinking the same thing. He was intently staring at gate eleven. He waved his hand, and a shimmering barrier appeared around us. It must be some magical protective dome. No one questioned it.

We were all used to Trez starting the meeting, but Trez just sat there looking at Grayson.

"Oh, right, I called this meeting," said Grayson awkwardly. "Well, for those of you who have just arrived, Isla just had her gatekeeper's stone stolen." Both Launch and Fynne looked like they were about to stand up and fight someone.

Grayson continued, "Obviously, this is very concerning, but the good thing is that we have a good idea where the attacks are coming from. I didn't mention this in the message I sent everyone but the person who originally attacked Wren ran back into gate eleven."

Even Jumana looked surprised by this, and nothing ever seemed to phase her.

"I chased him back in but was locked in. Launch saved me by breaking into the realm."

I could tell several gatekeepers had questions, but Grayson continued without pause. "They are clearly out to get gatekeeper stones. My main concern and reason for this meeting is our safety." He then turned to Isla. He seemed to be more confident. "We now have the issue of Isla's missing gatekeeper's stone. Evidently, whoever attacked her, jumped into her realm instead of going back to gate eleven, which I assume is where this person came from. As most of you know, the pirate realm is connected to the mermaid realm."

Fynne and even Launch nodded their heads like they already knew too. I looked at Via, and we both rolled our eyes. How do we miss these things?

"Trez," said Grayson. "I assume you have an extra gate key to get Isla back into your realm."

"Yes, but I do not possess a mermaid gate key so that she can turn into a mermaid to get to her realm."

Launch spoke up. "I actually think I have a couple working gate key gemstones for the mermaid realm," he said rather awkwardly. "I noticed them in the archives when I went and got the working gate keys for Wren. Or she could even take my gatekeeper stone."

"Oh, I wouldn't want to take your gatekeeper's stone," said Isla. "The gate keys would be perfect, though."

"Sounds good," said Trez. "Would anyone else like to volunteer to come with us to get Isla's stone back?"

"I will," said Grayson.

"I would like to go as well," I said.

"I would rather you stay," said Grayson matter of factly. "Especially with your injury. I can bring you back before we go, or you could hang out in your realm."

Demanding much? I huffed and sat back in my chair.

"Grayson is right, Wren," said Trez. "Besides, three of us

is probably plenty. We are up against only one person."

Fynne spoke up, "Wren, if you would like, you can come to my realm while you wait. The kids have missed you, and my wife would love to see you again."

I was bummed not to go on the mission, but I did love visiting Fynne and his family, so I agreed.

Chapter
9

We stepped through Fynne's gate and into the medieval realm's jousting arena. Fynne's gate was located at the far end of the arena on a massive stone platform where the winners of the tournaments would be announced. I went to one of those tournaments once, and it was like going to the most amazing renaissance festival you have ever been to; a day filled with turkey legs, flower crowns, and knights on horses.

We walked down the steps leading off the back of the platform and headed into the town towards Fynne's house, which was more like a stone mansion. It was located adjacent to the large castle that King Landon and Queen Ivory lived in. Much like my realm, the gatekeeper and the ruler of the realm were two separate jobs. Fynne was considered a knight and second in command.

We walked up to Fynne's estate, and suddenly three small children burst through the front door, followed by their mother, Joan.

Serena, the oldest, was the first to reach me. She was six years old and a total tomboy. "Wren, look at the wooden sword papa made for me!" She said, swinging it around with amazing control. Next came Blade, their adorable red-headed son who had just turned three. He was also carrying a wooden sword but dropped it when he saw me and sheepishly came up and hugged me. Lastly, little Nezetta, who was one and had just learned to walk, toddled up and held out her arms.

"Smells like we are in time for dinner," said Fynne as he came up to his wife and kissed her on the cheek.

"That you are," said Joan smiling. "Wren, I am so glad you could join us. We have all missed you. Blade has been asking for you recently."

I looked down at Blade, who was blushing but still looking at me with adoring eyes. I laughed and grabbed his hand as we walked through the tall wooden front doors and into their dining hall. Fynne, Joan, and I took a seat at the long wooden table, and I sat there for a moment, taking in the wonderful feeling of being a part of a bigger family. The kids were running around, warm food was being brought in, and Fynne was talking with Joan about his day. I loved the chaos of it all. I had always wished I had siblings growing up, and being with them was the closest thing to living that dream.

Nez started crying and began tugging on Joan's dress, making motions with her hands.

"You want food?" Said Joan grabbing a biscuit from the table and showing her.

Nez made a fist and nodded it up and down. Joan picked her up, put her in her little wooden seat at the table, and handed her the biscuit. I had forgotten that Fynne's family all knew sign language and used it frequently. No one in their family was deaf, so I always found it interesting that they even used sign language.

We stuffed our faces till we were full and all settled down near the large fireplace in their living room. After playing a few games with the kids and finding a book to read for a little bit, I suddenly had the urge to send Grayson a message to see how things were going. I contemplated whether or not I should send the message. I didn't want him to think I was being pushy, but at the same time, I really did want to know what was going on.

"Wren, are you ok?" Asked Joan. "You look unsettled."

I blushed. "Oh, it's nothing. I was just thinking of sending a message to Grayson."

Fynne overheard our conversation and chimed in. "Oh yes, please do. I would like to know how things are going."

"Ok, I'll do that then," I said, glad for the final push to

just do it. I quickly sent Grayson the message before I could overthink it. "Hey, Fynne and I just wanted to check in and see how things were going." I immediately thought that I should have added more to make it not seem like I was trying to rush him to come back when suddenly my gemstone lit up the deep red color of Grayson's realm, and I heard his response.

"Hey Wren, we figured out who has the gemstone and are coming up with a plan to get it back. We decided to stay the night and then try to retrieve it in the morning. Hopefully, I'll be back sometime tomorrow."

"Well, that sounds promising," said Fynne after relaying the message to him. "I'm glad they are ok. You are more than welcome to stay the night, Wren, or if you need to get back home, I can take you. Just let me know."

"If it's no trouble, I would love to stay the night," I said, knowing it was already getting really late. "I want to be here when they get back, and I don't have anything pressing at home." The kids cheered and dogpiled me. Joan sent one of the maids to go set up my room for me.

I sent a message back to Grayson saying that I was glad they were doing good and that I had decided to stay the night at Fynne's and would wait for them to get back. A minute later I got a message saying "Ok". Knowing Grayson, he probably wished he could just send the thumbs-up emoji.

The worries of Isla getting her stone back, the issues of my realm, and wondering if you could actually send an emoji using the gatekeeper stones kept me up most of the night. I finally fell asleep but woke up only a few hours later to the smell of the medieval realm's version of coffee and freshly baked breakfast scones. I made my way downstairs but stopped halfway when I received another message from Grayson.

"Hey Wren, we were able to get Isla's stone back. Trez and Isla are staying behind to help get everything back in order, but I am heading out now. If you want to meet me in the gate circle in five minutes, I'll take you home."

I finished making my way down the stairs and told Fynne what Grayson had said.

"Poor guy, he must be exhausted if they already got back the stone this early in the morning. Tell him to come in and grab some breakfast! I will open up the gate for him."

I messaged Grayson back, and he accepted the invitation. Twenty minutes later, he was sitting with us, scarfing down breakfast. He looked just as tired as me.

After Grayson had finished eating, Fynne spoke up.

"So how did it go, Grayson? Everyone safe and sound?"

"Yes," said Grayson, "It was actually a lot easier than we thought. I felt like the girl who stole the gemstone used it to bait us to come to her so she could steal our stones, but she underestimated our strength."

"Where is she now?" I asked.

"Trez is keeping her hostage in the pirate realm. Once we took the stone, she turned back into a human and started drowning, but we tied her hands together and strapped the gemstone back on her to get her to the surface. Once there, we took it back, and Trez locked her up."

Fynne stroked his beard. "Did she give you any information? Like why is she doing this, who is she working for?"

"No," said Grayson. He leaned back in his chair and rubbed his face in his hands. He was about to start talking again when suddenly there was a loud knock on the front door.

"Excuse me," said Fynne as he stood up to go check to see who it was. It felt like Fynne was barely gone before he suddenly burst back into the dining hall. "Joan, the dragon egg is hatching! Grab the kids. We have to head over now if we want to see it!"

Chapter 10

The house was in an uproar. Joan jumped up from the table and tried to pick up little Nez, who ran off thinking it was a game of chase. Fynne was darting around trying to find Blade's missing shoe, and Serina was loudly singing a song she had just made up about the dragon egg hatching.

"Sorry," said Fynne, who had finally found Blade's shoe and was putting it on his foot. "I guess I never told you, Wren, but we have had a dragon egg for what seems like centuries, and no one knew when or if it would hatch. You will have to excuse us. This is a once-in-a-lifetime experience. Feel free to join us, though! This is definitely something you will want to see."

I looked over at Grayson to see his reaction. He now looked like he was wide awake.

"I would love to come," Grayson said.

"I'm in too," I said

"Excellent! Let's get going!"

We all ran out of the house, the children were laughing, and Fynne and Joan were excitedly talking about what color they thought it would be. I was just excited to know that dragons existed in other realms, and maybe I could find out more about Kygra.

<hr />

We reached the castle and a Porter escorted us down to the room they kept the dragon egg in. It was a small ornate room with large tapestries with different scenes portraying dragons covering the walls. In the center was a large stone pedestal that looked more like an oven due to the fire burning inside of it. Resting on top in a divet carved into the stone was the egg. It was jet black but shimmered in the firelight from the torches on the wall. There was a large crack down the middle of it, and every once in a while, it was rock as the dragon tried to break free. King Landon and Queen Ivory were there as well with their family.

"Fynne, how did this dragon egg come into your realm's possession? I thought I was the only one who had a dragon in their realm," I said.

Grayson looked directly at me. "You have a dragon in your realm?"

"Well, yes. She lives on an island just off the mainland

across from the wood elf village."

"How long has she been there?" he asked, with one eyebrow raised.

"She showed up the same time my father disappeared."

He stood there, looking deep in thought.

Fynne spoke up after Grayson didn't continue. "Well, to answer your question Wren, it was discovered during my grandfather's time by a girl who wandered deep in Wyvern Woods. It was said that dragons used to be common long ago but slowly disappeared because they were hunted for sport. So you can imagine the excitement when it was discovered. Taking care of it has become a time-honored tradition and the title of dragon keeper is one that is highly esteemed."

I nodded and then looked back over at Grayson, who was still deep in thought. "Grayson, are you ok?"

"Me? Yes, I am fine," he said, shaking off the dazed look on his face.

My eyes drifted to the tapestry on the walls. I realized these must have been scenes from back when the dragons were hunted in the realm. One portrayed a knight fighting a green dragon, and another portrayed a knight holding the head of another dragon. But upon further investigation, I noticed one tapestry in the back of the room that depicted a beautiful woman with her hand held up. Another tapestry blocked the other half of the image. I walked up and moved the tapestry on top to reveal a dragon on the other side. It was leaning its head down towards the woman, and the woman's hand was resting on the bridge of its nose. Both had their eyes closed and were smiling. It was a stark difference between the other tapestries full of death and severed dragon heads. I continued to study the tapestry and noticed that around the edges of the tapestry were symbols that looked familiar. I remembered the piece of paper we had found in Kygra's cave. I pulled it out of my satchel to compare. It was definitely the same writing. Suddenly I heard Grayson's voice whisper directly behind me.

"What is that you got there?" He asked mysteriously. I jumped and turned around.

"Oh, umm, just this." I handed him the paper. "Root and I found this in Kygra's cave last time we went."

He studied it intently, comparing it to the tapestry.

"Have you ever heard your dragon speak?" he asked.

"No, why would she?" I asked, confused. "Wait, do dragons talk?"

"Sometimes," replied Grayson, still studying the paper.

"What do you mean sometimes?" I sighed.

He didn't respond.

"Do you know how to read that?" I asked instead.

"Not really," he said, not even bothering to look up at me. A voice behind us interrupted my angry thoughts of punching Grayson.

"What do you have there?" asked the little old dragon keeper. I snatched the paper out of Grayson's hand, glad to have someone who might actually answer my questions.

"I noticed that this writing and the writing on this tapestry match," I said, handing the paper to him.

"Well, what you have here is dragon language," said the dragon keeper after studying it for a moment.

"Dragon language, can you read it?"

"Oh no," said the man handing it back to me. "It's a forgotten language. The only reason I know its dragon language is because my father told me that is what the symbols on this tapestry were. This was made back during a time when humans and dragons were under friendlier terms. Apparently, dragons could talk then and had a language of their own."

I turned to Grayson, and he just shrugged.

Suddenly there was a commotion behind us, and we both turned around just in time to see the baby dragon emerge from its egg. It was a deep teal color and had piercing dark red eyes. It then opened its mouth and yawned the cutest yawn I have ever seen in my life. This caused all the kids to squeal and clamber towards it. Surprisingly the adults let the children pet it, even little Nez, who was basically the same size as it.

"Wren, would you like to pet it?" asked Fynne after the kids had had their turn. I walked up, Grayson trailing behind me, and reached my hand out to pet the top of its head. The tiny scales that covered its body were so smooth. It was now lying down, tired from all the commotion. I then went to stroke its back and feel its soft leathery wings, but it reared its head, and then an explosion of little sparks flew out its nose. I immediately retracted my hand, but then I laughed, realizing it was just a sneeze, and reached out to pet it once again.

Grayson came up beside me and petted the dragon as well. He was standing so close our shoulders were touching. I would usually pull away, but instead, I stayed right where I was. My breathing started getting shallow, and I couldn't focus on anything else. Grayson was enamored with the dragon and didn't seem to notice. I was so distracted that I had stopped petting it and just stared.

Grayson looked over at me and must have seen the glazed-over look on my face. "Oh, sorry," he said, stepping away.

I blushed, realizing he didn't mean to be touching my shoulder. Or did he? I don't know.

⸻ ❦ ⸻

We stayed a little longer to watch the dragon trainer take the dragon to its new home near the stable yard. Once there, the adults launched into a lengthy conversation about what they should name it. They finally decided upon Burgan. It was a little formal for my taste, but it was the name of King Landon's great great great grandfather or something like that, so I kept my opinion to myself.

The excitement died down, and I could now tell Grayson was getting tired. I was ready to head back home too. We dropped off Joan and the kids back at their house, and

Fynne walked us back to his gate.

"Wren, I was wondering if I could visit the dragon in your realm at some point. Your dragon is the only other known dragon in all of the realms, so I would like to see her for myself. Maybe I can learn something to help us with our dragon."

"Of course!" I responded.

"I would like to see her as well," said Grayson casually.

I wanted to say no and yell at him for clearly hiding information from me, but instead, I was a wimp and responded, "No problem, then let's plan a time to all go together." Internally I was kicking myself in the face.

Grayson and I went through the gate, him going first to make sure no one was out there. I went through after him, and when the coast was clear, we made our way back to where we had parked our cars.

"Soooo," I said after we'd walked in silence for a little bit. "Can you read the dragon's language? You uh, seem to know a lot about it."

Grayson sighed. "No, I can't read it," He seemed slightly annoyed.

"You sure?" I asked, pushing it further. "Or is there something you know that I should know?"

He kept walking, staring straight ahead, not bothering to look at me. "I am positive I don't know dragon language,

Wren."

"You are dodging around something, and I want to know what it is!"

Still, he didn't turn around.

That was it. I grabbed his shoulder and spun him around to face me. I realized I was exhausted, my emotions were super high at this point, but I didn't care. I was sick of feeling like I was in the dark when it came to Grayson, especially since there seemed to be some sort of tension between us.

"Please," I pleaded, "I feel like I don't even know you, and if we are going to keep doing this together, I need to know I can trust you." Tears started to well in my eyes. Grayson just stood there, staring at me. I felt like an idiot.

"Wren, I..."

His voice sounded different as he said that, but then he stopped. I looked up at him. Concern was written all over his face. He took a step closer to me. His face relaxed, and he shook his head as if to clear some thought from his brain.

"I really have nothing else to say. I was just curious, that's all," he said, his voice cold and calculated. I didn't believe a word of it. He looked like he was about to say something else, stopped himself, turned to leave, and then turned back once more. He awkwardly put his hand on my shoulder and patted me like a lost puppy.

"But, uhh, it's going to be ok," He clearly had never

consoled someone in his life.

    The rest of our trip back was spent in silence, other than him saying goodbye. After I made it back home, I ran up to my apartment and crashed on my bed. I was so frustrated, especially with myself. Was I making up things in my head, or was Grayson really hiding things from me. I felt like he was someone I shouldn't be trusting, but I wanted to trust him so badly. I also found myself just wanting to be around him all the time, to be able to talk to him openly about things, share my feelings with him. But if he was keeping things from me, I should want to keep my distance, right? Frustrated, I buried my head in my pillow and attempted to fall asleep.

Chapter
11

I spent the next couple of days working on my business, restocking my shop, getting caught up on orders, and making more videos. It was nice to have something to do to keep my mind off of things.

Everything came crashing back when Grayson texted me and let me know that Trez called another meeting. We decided to go visit Kygra with Fynne right after the meeting, which worked out perfectly since it was my normal time to visit. Grayson met me at our parking spot and walked with me to the gate circle as usual. We didn't say anything the whole time. Since Grayson wasn't willing to share things, I felt there was some invisible wall between us that I wasn't sure how to navigate around it.

When we arrived, Fynne was at his gate, allowing everyone to enter. Because of the present danger, we had decided to meet in Fynne's realm. We were the last ones to arrive. Everyone else was already sitting at the long wooden table that Fynne had set up just inside his gate on the large stone podium overlooking the entire jousting arena. Fynne took a seat at the head of the table, and Grayson and I took the last two remaining seats, which happened to be next to each other.

Great.

I looked over at Via, who was sitting on the other side of me. She just smiled at me and winked. I rolled my eyes and looked away. I was not in the mood.

"Alright," said Trez, who was sitting at the head of the table opposite of Fynne. "A lot has happened in the past several days, and I want to catch you all up. We seem to be the enemy of gate eleven. Although it has been dangerous, the one good thing is that we know that gate eleven gatekeeper's stone is within the realm. Although this gets us one step closer to obtaining all the gatekeeper stones, unfortunately, it now poses a threat that needs to be taken care of." Trez shifted in his seat. "Now, we clearly know that Wren's attacker was from realm eleven, and I do believe Isla's attacker is from there as well. We have tried to have discussions with her but unfortunately, she hasn't divulged any pertinent information. The only thing we do know about her is that she can manipulate natural elements and carried this stone with her." Trez reached into his pocket and pulled out a stone that looked exactly like our own gatekeeper stones except it was solid black. Even as Trez held it up in the sunlight, no light could be seen through it.

Grayson shifted in his chair but didn't say anything. I looked over at him, and he seemed concerned, or maybe angry, I couldn't tell. I looked back at the stone Trez held out and wondered why Grayson said nothing about this when he explained everything in Fynne's realm. Maybe he just didn't know she had it? Who am I kidding? He probably knew.

Via spoke up beside me. "What is that?"

"That is a good question," said Trez looking at Grayson, who seemed to suddenly be preoccupied with a loose thread on the sleeve of his shirt. "We have no idea, but it seems to hinder magic rather than amplify it like our own gatekeeper stones. I have kept it locked up in my realm for now."

Grayson mumbled something under his breath.

"You good?" I whispered to him

"Just fine," he grumbled back. I looked over at Via, and she just shrugged and then pointed at Isla, who was looking slightly terrified at Grayson.

Trez continued, "It apparently can take the magic from a gate key gemstone as we witnessed in Isla's realm. Now you can only imagine what this could cause in the mermaid realm since you need your magic to breathe underwater, but fortunately, no one was killed, thanks to Grayson."

I stared, blinking at Grayson. His personality became more and more of a mystery. Frustrated didn't even begin to come close to describing how I felt.

"So, let's start talking about how we can defend ourselves and what steps we can take to stop this. First, thank you, Fynne, for allowing us to use your realm as our new meeting place. Until the threat is gone, I would like to continue meeting inside our realms, rather than the gate circle."

We all nodded.

"My next suggestion is to always be accompanied by someone else when leaving your realms, especially for those who live outside of the realms." He gestured towards Grayson and me. "Lastly, I would like to experiment with the dark stone to see if there are ways of defending against it. I have a few of my men working on it now, and I will update you once we find out more. Other than that, does anyone have any further questions?" He looked directly at Grayson. There was a long awkward pause. Grayson still seemed to be preoccupied with his sleeve.

"Continuing on then," said Trez, "As far as we all know, we really don't know what realm eleven contains. From the description I received from Grayson and Launch, there really wasn't much to see, am I correct."

When Grayson didn't say anything, Launch finally

spoke up. "Well, umm.. gate eleven seems to be a pretty generic realm. But one thing I forgot to mention was that there seemed to be five different sections. The gate to the realm is located in the center of those five sections."

"What do you mean by sections?" asked Trez.

"Well, I just noticed as I was flying in to get to Grayson that there was a stark difference in the characteristics of the land below which made it look like five different colors. I assumed the differences to be different types of landscapes and architectural features. What the exact differences were, I couldn't say."

Trez nodded, deep in thought. "Interesting," he said. "Launch, do you think you could get us back into the realm?"

"As I was telling Wren and Via, due to me having to prepare a new ship and charge more sunstones, I would need approximately four months to get everything ready to go."

Trez scratched his head. "Well, unfortunately, that does not help us," He paused. "But if you could get started on that, at least it could be our backup plan if all else fails."

Launch nodded.

"Already started," he said. "I was very excited it actually worked, considering I wasn't fully prepared for it. I made some adjustments on the new ship to compensate for some shortcomings on the previous ship, so we shouldn't have any issues this second time around."

"Perfect," said Trez. "Grayson, do you have anything to

add?"

Grayson shook his head.

It made me angry knowing that Grayson could probably help, but for some reason, he was refusing. What happened to the guy that jumped to my assistance when I needed more gate key gemstones!

I was so upset I didn't even really remember the rest of the meeting. The only thing I did notice was Isla. She looked uncomfortable the whole meeting. I decided that I was going to talk to her afterward. She seems like the girl who would spill her guts, unlike mister mind of a thousand deadlocks over here.

The meeting finally ended, and I walked up to Isla, who jumped when I said her name.

"Sorry. I didn't mean to scare you. Everything ok?"

Isla quickly glanced over at Grayson, who was still sitting in his seat waiting to go to my realm. She turned her back to him and leaned in closer to me. "I am a little worried about Grayson,"

"What, why?"

"Well, I mean, he did save some of my friends, so he seems like a good person. But something happened to cause me to question him."

"What happened?"

"Well," she said, "When we finally captured Ava, oh that's her name, by the way, the lady who tried to take over my realm. Anyway, when Trez took my gatekeeper's stone back and found the black stone, Grayson said that he would take the black stone and keep it safe. Trez said that he had a really good place to hide it, so he would keep it. They got into a huge argument, but in the end, Trez won. I am not sure why Grayson would fight so hard to keep that stone, especially since it seems evil. I guess I am just confused where he stands with everything."

"Tell me about it," I muttered.

"What?" said Isla.

"Nothing," I said. My brain was spinning. I had no idea what side Grayson was on. And here I was, letting him in my realm again. I turned back to Isla.

"No need to worry," I told her. "I will keep an eye on him. Thank you for telling me."

"I am glad I have you to talk to." She smiled and let out a sigh of relief. "You should come to visit my realm sometime!"

"I would love that," I smiled back.

"Love what?" Came a voice from behind me. By the look on Isla's face, I knew right away who it was.

Isla nervously answered before I could respond. "Oh, just that she would love to visit my realm sometime."

"Great," said Grayson. "Well, you ready to go?" he asked impatiently.

"Just give me a second," I snapped. "Besides, we have to wait for Fynne who is still talking to Trez. So go sit back down or something, and maybe you can fix whatever is wrong with your sleeve you have been so preoccupied with."

He stood there blinking at me. I half expected him to fight back, but instead, he did exactly what I said and sat back down in his seat. Isla looked at me in pure awe.

༺✦༻

After a few more minutes, Fynne finished talking to Trez, and we all left to go to my gate. Via ended up coming because she invited herself, and to be honest, I was glad. The more people we had, the safer I felt with Grayson. We stepped through the gate and Root met us. I never got to tell him that I had guests coming this time and had a look of shock on his face.

"Wren, what's going on?" He asked.

"Ok, it's a long story, but they are all here to check out Kygra because Fynne has a dragon that hatched in his realm, and he wants to see if he could learn more about them by observing Kygra."

"Ok," said Root. "So why is Grayson here?"

"Well, he happened to be with us when the dragon hatched, and he asked if he could come too."

"Oh, and then you just couldn't say no, is that it?" He said mockingly with a big grin that I immediately wanted to smack off his face. I was over people teasing me about Grayson.

"Ok, you know what, I have been a little concerned about him, and if you could keep a close eye on him, that would be great," I said frustratedly.

Root became serious. "Are you ok? What did he do?"

"I'll explain everything on the way down," I replied.

"Everything ok," came Fynne's voice from behind us.

"Oh yes, totally fine," I said, smiling. "Root was just saying that he would love to take us to go see Kygra."

"Great!" Said Fynne, "Let's get going, shall we?"

⁂

During our journey, I filled Root in on everything that happened in the mermaid realm and the new suspicions about the dark stone we had discovered. He stayed by Grayson's side after that, but I could tell he was confused by the fact that the guy who was able to help us calm down the dwarf king was now back on the watch list. I was getting exhausted from keeping up with all the back and forth myself.

We made great time, and by mid-day, we found ourselves just outside Kygra's cave. We were in luck. She happened to be just inside the mouth of the cave, resting. Via started hyperventilating out of pure excitement, Fynne took out a notebook and started taking notes, and Grayson had pulled up his sleeve and, for some reason, was fumbling with his gatekeeper stone that was strapped to his wrist, just like mine. This was new. He must have copied me. I looked over at Root, who was staring at Grayson.

"You got a problem? Asked Grayson, briefly looking up from his wrist.

"Do you?" Responded Root.

Just then, Via jumped out from behind the boulder we were hiding behind.

"Come on, guys, let's go check her out!" Via seemed to be immune to fear, often getting herself in trouble. Grayson grabbed her arm and jerked her back behind the boulder. Root jumped up, grabbing the hilt of his sword.

"Wait," said Grayson before Root could draw the sword on him, "I'm sorry, that was a little rough," He said, putting his hands up. "Before we all go to the cave though, I want to try something first."

"Try what?" Said Root, clearly getting more defensive.

"This," He said as he held out his arm. He closed his eyes, and then suddenly, his gemstone changed from its normal dark crimson color to a light green color. Grayson opened his eyes as a loud roar came from the cave.

Chapter
12

Absolute chaos ensued. Root jumped at Grayson and tried wrestling the gatekeeper stone off of his wrist. Via immediately went into asking a million questions even though no one was really listening. Fynne, who finally looked up from his writing, half-heartedly tried to stop Grayson and Root from fighting.

My mind was racing. The light green color was the color of gate five. So did Grayson just send a message to the gatekeeper of gate five? I looked up and watched as Kygra ran around her cave as if she was searching for someone. It suddenly clicked.

"Is Kygra the gatekeeper to realm five?" I said, still in utter shock.

Everyone went silent. Root let go of Grayson. Fynne,

Via, and Root stared at me.

Grayson looked impressed and then brushed himself off. "Yes," he said matter of factly. "Way to go, Sherlock Holmes."

"Wait, what?" stuttered Root. Via still hadn't said anything, which was unusual for her. Fynne looked very deep in thought. Grayson stood up.

"You all stay here. I am going to talk to her." He spun around and started walking towards the cave. I ran after him, Via trailing behind me. Kygra suddenly stopped, her eyes fixed on us. She crouched as if she was about to pounce on us like a cat. As we got closer, she noticed me and growled. Via and I both stopped in our tracks, but Grayson kept making his way towards her as if nothing was wrong. He stopped directly in front of her. His aggressive approach made her sit back on her haunches, now looking like a dog. He closed his eyes, and once again, the stone on his wrist turned light green. Kygra cocked her head to one side and then slowly stood on all fours once again.

"Does she not understand you?" I asked. "Maybe she only speaks whatever language the dragon keeper was talking about, you know, on the paper?" I was fumbling to get it out of my bag. I had just pulled it out and went to look back up at Kygra, but instead of a dragon, there was a small woman with messy jet black hair marching towards me.

"That," she said as she snatched the paper out of my hands, "is mine, thank you very much."

She looked over the paper for a moment. "Oh, and by the way, I understand you perfectly," she said, shoving the paper into the pocket of her light green kimono. "Don't know why you all keep visiting me. I have been perfectly fine on my own." She turned to go back into her cave. "By the way, who are you?" she said, spinning around and marching towards me once again. "You're the new gatekeeper to this realm, right? What happened to Ardon?"

"Ardon?" I said, "You mean my father?" It felt odd to hear a complete stranger mention my father's name.

"He is your father?" growled Kygra, stopping in her tracks. Her face was fixed in a menacing glare. She started slowly walking towards me.

Grayson and Root took steps closer to me. I held up my hand to keep them back.

"What did my father ever do to you?" I asked.

"What did he do to me?" Kygra scoffed. "Trapped me here; that's what he did. He promised he would help me and then two days later vanished. I have been stuck in this fairy-infested princess realm ever since."

"I am sorry," I responded, taking a step closer to her. "We are here now, and we want to help you. We can take you back to your realm." Kygra glanced nervously from person to person and took a step back.

"Well, to be honest, I am not sure I want to go back after all," she said. "I left for a reason, and I am not sure I would be welcomed back. Especially after I stole the gatekeeper stone."

"You stole it?" I said.

"Yes, that is literally what I just said."

"So you don't want to go back?"

"I mean, it would be nice to see my family again. It's been what? 25 years?"

"Wait, how old are you?" asked Grayson.

"Let's see. I left my realm when I was 17, so that would make me about 42, I guess."

"What?" I said. "You don't look a day over 20."

"Oh, good!" She said, "I heard that one of the perks of transforming into a dragon is that it stops aging because dragons age much slower than humans. Glad to know it's true," She straightened her hair and patted down her kimono.

"So do you want to go or not," said Grayson.

I nudged him in the shoulder.

"What?"

I huffed in exasperation.

"Ok, I want to go," said Kygra, interrupting.

"Great!" said Grayson.

"But first, who are the rest of you? I only recognize this one," said Kygra, pointing to Root.

"Oh yes, sorry, the one you already know is Root. He is my protector here in Lustria. Then there is Grayson, who is the gatekeeper for realm six. Next is Via; she is from the steampunk realm, and then lastly we have Fynne, from the medieval realm."

Kygra suddenly took multiple steps back and looked horrified.

"The medieval realm?" She yelled, "They used to collect our kind and then hunt and kill us for sport! That's it. I'm staying." She took off running to the back of her cave again.

"Kygra, wait!" I called after her. "Don't worry. They no longer hunt dragons. In fact, Fynne is here to see if he could find more information on how to take care of them." Her curiosity won the better of her, and she started walking back. "You see, they have a dragon egg that has finally hatched after all these years, and they need to know what it needs to keep it healthy. As a matter of fact, Fynne would probably be very grateful if you went to his realm to help him. After we figure everything out with your realm, of course." This seemed to calm Kygra down.

Fynne spoke up. "Yes, I would be honored if you came to help us with our little one."

She looked back and forth between all of us. "Alright, let's go. I am ready to get out of here," She said, walking out of the cave.

"Wow, Grayson, she is almost as bipolar as you," said Via, hitting Grayson on the shoulder as we followed Kygra out. Grayson just scowled. I laughed. Kygra suddenly turned around again.

"What now?" said Grayson, clearly perturbed.

"If you don't mind, I am going to follow you guys as a bird. Human legs aren't my favorite." In the blink of an eye, she turned into a little sparrow. We all stood there staring.

"What do you think the theme of her realm is? I think it must have something to do with animals, just a hunch," Via whispered to me sarcastically.

"That's a pretty good hunch you got there." I laughed. "Guess we will find out!"

Chapter
13

"I am so glad you all decided to spend the night at the castle," said Falveron to Kygra as we all sat around the table in the large dining hall back at the castle. We realized it was getting late and decided to stay in Luma for the night on the way back.

At first, Kygra didn't seem to like the idea, but as soon as we mentioned food, she was totally fine with it.

"And what a pleasant surprise to meet you again, Kygra, and in your human form too! I had no idea you could transform." continued Falveron.

Kygra was very preoccupied with her food, which she immediately started eating like a wild animal as soon as it came out. At first, it was a little repulsive, but if I was honest with myself, that is exactly how I would eat my first real meal in 25 years too.

"Nice to meet you again, too," she finally responded through a full mouth of potatoes and turkey leg.

"You know, I had gone back once to find you after Ardon left. Obviously, I didn't find you though, you must have been hiding in your cave," said Falveron.

"That was nice of you," said Kygra, clearly way more interested in her food than in conversation. She finished only moments later and then spent the rest of the meal nodding off to sleep and jerking her head up to keep herself awake.

"Kygra, if you are tired, I could show you to your room for the night if you would like?" I finally asked.

"That would be great," She said, jumping up from her seat as if she was suddenly wide awake. She practically ran out, not saying goodnight to anyone. I had to jog to keep up with her. We made it out the first doorway, and she turned the corner and let out a huge sigh.

"What's wrong, Kygra?" I asked, "Are you ok?"

"Oh yes," She said. "That is the most people I have been around in, well forever, and I don't know about you, but being around that many new aura's can be exhausting."

"I'm sorry, new what?" I said.

"Auras," repeated Kygra "You know, the essence your soul gives off. We also sometimes call it vibes."

"Seriously?" I said

"Yes, why? Do you know the term vibes?"

I chuckled. "It means something a little different where I am from."

"Interesting," said Kygra. "But anyway, I can sense the innermost part of people's souls. Not that I can read minds, I can just get a general sense of whether people are genuinely good or not, you know? Like their overall feeling. I just forgot how overwhelming it can be."

"What is my aura?" I asked, intrigued.

"Yours is good," she said flatly.

"Then why did you react the way you did to me initially back at the cave when you mentioned my father? Was his Aura bad?"

"No, your father's aura was good as well. You both have very similar aura's actually, mostly good mixed with a little bit of confusion."

I wanted to deny the confusion part but realized it was true.

"But I have learned that even if one's aura is good, that doesn't necessarily mean that person will make good decisions." continued Kygra, glancing at me. "So naturally, I have a hard time trusting people even if I do know their aura. But the sense of all your aura's together is overwhelmingly positive, especially that Grayson fellow."

"Grayson?" I asked.

"Yes, the moody one with the bright hair."

Yup, that was Grayson.

"He has a lot of things swirling around in that aura of his, more than most people, but his intentions are one of the purest I have ever felt."

I was shocked by this news and had more questions, but Kygra immediately changed the subject and started commenting on the pictures on the wall and the strange color of the curtains.

We got to her room that the maids had made up for her, and Kygra ran in.

"This is great!" She said, "Nice and big, perfect, goodnight!" She suddenly turned back into a dragon, causing the furniture surrounding her to screech in protest, her large dragon body pushing them out of the way. She then circled and curled up like a dog and instantly fell asleep.

I laughed and shook my head. I have never met such an odd person in my life. I watched as puffs of smoke rose from her nostrils each time she snored, and I suddenly felt super tired myself and decided to turn in.

Bright and early the next morning we prepared to leave. We had a quick breakfast in the kitchen. Root was a little on edge and kept glancing over at Grayson, who didn't seem to notice at all. We finished up, and I was just about to make my way to the courtyard to get ready to go when Root pulled me into one of the side rooms off of the main entrance.

"Root, what's wrong?" I asked. "Are you ok? You seem off."

"I just wanted to talk in private with you before you all left. It really bothers me that Grayson is tagging along." He said.

"I mean, I get it. I am a little concerned myself, especially how he just jumped into the whole thing with Kygra without telling us. But Fynne and Via will be there. And if he planned on hurting me, I think he would have done it by now. I don't know. I am probably just as confused as you." I looked down at the floor to avoid Root's eyes. I didn't want him to see I was confused about more than just Grayson's allegiance.

Root sighed and shifted his stance. "Well, I am glad Fynne and Via are going. Probably wouldn't let you go without them. Just please," He said as he grabbed my hands, "please be careful."

I stared at our hands. My heart suddenly started racing.

"Wren, there is another reason I don't like him going with you," he whispered. He took a step closer to me. I looked up, his face close to mine. He started to slowly lean in towards me. What was he doing? We were just friends, right?

"Wren, I-"

"Fynne's ready to go," interrupted Grayson suddenly at the doorway. Root took a step back from me. My head was spinning too much to say anything. Via appeared in the doorway as well. "Come on, Wren! I am so excited to see what Kygra's realm looks like!"

"Coming!" I said as I passed Root to get to the door, trying to clear the haze in my brain. "Bye, Root," I said as naturally as I could. "I will tell you all about it when I get back."

Root suddenly grabbed my hand and pulled me in for a hug. "Please just keep your eyes open, will you?" He whispered in my ear. He pulled away and looked at me, brows furrowed in concern. He then looked up at Grayson. The look of concern was gone and had been replaced by a stare that could kill.

"Let's get going, shall we?" I said to Grayson, trying to diffuse the tension. I walked out the door, and Grayson slowly turned and followed me. My mind was reeling over the whole thing but not for long because before I knew it, we were at the gate circle getting ready to enter the unknown realm of gate five.

Chapter
~ 14 ~

Kygra stood in front of her gate, staring at it for an uncomfortable amount of time.

Via looked over at me. I shrugged. Via opened her mouth to say something, but the words never came.

Kygra abruptly turned around and faced us, letting out a long sigh. "Ok, my realm's gate opens up in the main hub. We will be safe there as long as nothing has drastically changed in the twenty-five years I have been gone. Hopefully, my parents are still alive. Otherwise, this might be a little umm... Well, tense... we should be fine."

"Gosh, what are we getting ourselves into?" whispered Via.

"I don't know," I said. "For someone who talks a lot, she really doesn't give much information."

Without any further explanation, Kygra opened her gate and walked right in. The rest of us rushed to follow.

Nothing could have prepared me for what I saw. Via and I both gasped when we walked in, and Grayson even let out a "wow." We stood on a large elevated stone platform. Staircases to the right and the left lead down to a circular stone plateau, much like the one that the gates stood on, except instead of forest surrounding it, there was a deep moat. Continual waterfalls flowed down from both sides, the mist from them swirling up from below. Past the moat, we were surrounded by six different landscapes, each having a bridge that led over the moat to them. Directly in front of us was what seemed to be the arctic, covered in snow and glaciers. Following that was a forest, thick with trees, rivers, and waterfalls, like the forests in my realm. Next was desert, sprawling sand dunes dotted with the occasional oasis. Directly behind us was a menacing-looking mountain range with the bridge leading into a dark valley. Definitely not the first place I would want to visit here. Then came a rainforest with giant trees with long vines hanging from them, thick foliage below. The last one was an island paradise, sprawling white beaches, and an ocean glistening in the distance.

"Welcome to Nageri, the animal realm," said Kygra.

"Called it," Via whispered to me. It suddenly all clicked as I heard beards chirping from the forest realm, monkeys chattering from the rainforest realm, and I am pretty sure I saw a dolphin breach in the tropical realm. I also realized there was not a human in sight. The beauty of it all suddenly became eerie.

"Come on, everyone," said Kygra as she made her way to one of the staircases and descended. We followed. The staircase hugged the side of a large building of some kind. The staircase ended in front of giant wooden double doors that led inside of it.

"Would you all like to find out what animals you would turn into in my realm?" asked Kygra. No one said anything, which I assumed was because we were all trying to wrap our heads around exactly what Kygra just asked of us.

Kygra seemed to notice our confusion. "So here in my realm, you can become your soul's animal at will. There is also another option where you have to stay human, but you can pick whatever animal you would like as your familiar. Most people choose to transform into an animal, though, which is what we are going to do now. I am assuming since you all have gatekeeper stones it will let you perform the Soulsera." We all stood there blinking, still trying to take in what she was telling us. "Just follow me."

With the help of Grayson and Fynne, she opened the wooden doors. A large domed room spread out before us. Straight ahead in the back of the room were steps leading up to a platform that contained a stone dragon hand reaching up out of it and clutching a glowing orb. Other than the orb, the room was completely empty. I looked up and noticed that there were animals painted on the ceiling. Lions, bears, snakes, birds, every possible animal you could imagine. The biggest was a large dragon painted just behind the glowing orb. Its head arched above and looked down at the glowing orb, its giant wings spread out behind it. One of its hands was grabbing the edge where the wall met the floor, and the other disappeared below. I then realized the stone hand clutching the orb was actually an extension of the painting and was the missing arm.

"Alright, Wren, how about you go first," said Kygra, who was suddenly by my side. "All you need to do is hold your gatekeeper's gemstone against your chest, be sure it's in contact with your skin, and place your other hand on the glowing sphere up there." She nodded towards the orb.

"But wait, what happens after that?" I asked nervously.

"You will transfer into your souls animal," said Kygra

"But how do I change back?"

"You'll feel it," she said, as she gave me a nudge towards the platform. Her vagueness was not comforting.

I made it halfway across the room before I stopped and turned around. "Can you just come with me?"

"Usually, people perform their Soulsera all by themselves in here because you never know what animal they are going to turn into. For example, if you turn into an elephant or a whale, there is a good chance we could get hurt if we stand too close."

I nodded, feeling even more terrified. I walked the rest of the way across the room, trying to keep myself from shaking. I made it to the platform and walked up the steps, taking my gatekeeper's stone off my wrist as I went. I pushed the flat side against my heart and positioned myself directly in front of the orb. The orb itself was mesmerizing to watch. It was so bright it took a moment for my eyes to focus. When they did I could make out faint colors swirling and moving in random directions and at different speeds, like it was alive. The light danced through my fingers as I reached out and set my hand on what felt like warm glass. That is when my gatekeeper stone disappeared into my chest. I panicked and let go of the sphere but not before I felt my feet leave the ground. My whole body seemed to be glowing, and the colors that once swirled in the sphere were now swirling around me. A bright light flashed and I felt myself falling. I panicked and started flapping my arms for stability, waiting for my body to make an impact on the floor but it never happened. I slowly opened my eyes, still flapping my arms which I now realized were covered with feathers and that I was, in fact, flying. I had become a bird and a small one at that.

Everything was now significantly bigger, including the orb, which was now twice my size. I turned around and started to fly back to the group. Just as I reached them, I had the thought that I wanted to turn back into a human, and it happened instantaneously. I wasn't prepared, though, and ended up face planting on the cold stone floor, my gatekeeper's stone skidding away from me.

"Smooth," said Grayson as Kygra helped me back up. Via was cracking some joke about how ironic it was that I had turned into an actual wren, but I wasn't really listening because I was too focused on glaring at Grayson as I brushed myself off.

"You'll get used to it," said Kygra, laughing. "You also need to be prepared to grab your gatekeeper's stone when transforming as well." She picked up my stone from the floor. "It becomes a part of you when you transform into an animal, but when you change back, it will appear just over your chest once again. That's why I wear a special harness that keeps my gatekeeper stone in place. You would hate to lose your gemstone after transforming back". She pressed her robe down on her sternum to show the outline of her gatekeeper's stone.

"Alright, next?" said Kygra. Via got excited and practically ran across the room. Before I knew it, there was another bright flash of light, and instead of an animal appearing, Via completely disappeared.

"Kygra!" I yelled frantically, looking around. "What happened? Where is Via?" I started running across the room towards the orb.

"STOP!" Yelled Kygra. I immediately listened. "She could be a very tiny creature, and you wouldn't want to crush her. Just give her a moment."

I froze in place, scanning the floor. Movement caught

my eye, and a little mouse came running up to me. I squealed and fell backward, trying to get away from it. The mouse suddenly turned into a laughing Via who helped me up off the ground.

"I can't believe I am a mouse." She laughed. "I always thought that it would be cool to travel through little nooks and crannies of the old houses in the steampunk realm, so this is great!"

"Glad you like it," I said, brushing myself off once again. This was too much excitement for one day.

I heard Fynne chuckle behind me and say, "Ok, my turn."

As Fynne walked up to the orb, Kygra turned around and stared out the doors. "Uh, continue on. I will be right back." Concern etched on her face. She turned back into the little bird she had transformed into before and flitted out the door.

Another flash of light filled the room and a magnificent chestnut-colored horse stood before us. Fynne trotted around the room and reared on his hind legs before turning back into a human. "I think I am going to like this realm," he said, walking back up to us. "Where did Kygra go?"

"She turned into a bird and left," said Via, pointing out the door. "She said she would be right back, though."

Fynne scratched his beard and went to look out the doors.

Via and I turned around to look at Grayson, who was

the last one left. He shrugged his shoulders and walked across the room. He placed his hand on the orb, which seemed to be taking its time. It started pulsing, the light slowly exiting it and wrapping itself around his arm, then his torso, then down his other arm to where he held his gatekeeper's stone against his chest. Then finally came the flash of light, followed by a rush of wind so strong I had to close my eyes. When I opened them again, my heart almost leaped out of its chest. There, standing before us, was Grayson, who was now a giant, fire-breathing dragon.

Chapter 15

We all stood there staring. In dragon form, Grayson was slightly bigger than Kygra. He was a very light gray, but his right front arm was pitch black. The discoloration slowly faded into gray as it went up his arm. His dark red eyes really stood out against his light coloring and they appeared to be glowing. Grayson seemed just as surprised as us. He was slowly looking over his new form but stopped when he came to his black arm.

"Time to leave," came Kygra's voice directly behind us. Via and I jumped.

"Oh, Grayson, you have a dragon's soul. Congratulations. That is rare, very rare. That technically means you could be the Alpha, I mean gatekeeper, in this realm. Not that you would want to." She mumbled the last part and started shuffling us out.

"Kygra, what happened?" asked Fynne, as Kygra was shoving him out the door.

"Oh nothing," she said nervously. "It's fine. You just all need to leave immediately, that's all. Dragon boy, please turn back into a human... NOW!" She yelled, half-crazed.

Grayson quickly obeyed and joined us. She shuffled us back up the stairs mumbling some sort of nonsense that I did not understand. I took a second to look around, wondering what on earth was suddenly so wrong, but everything looked exactly as it did when we first came in.

We made it to the top, and Kygra opened up the gate. In a flash, she turned back into a dragon, and with one swoop of her claw, she pushed us all simultaneously out the door. We landed in a heap just outside, Grayson to my left, Via and Fynne to my right. I didn't even have time to sit up before Kygra's head appeared through the gate now in human form.

"Sorry, just got a few things to take care of. If you need me, just send one of those message thingys." She paused as if she was deep in thought. "Ok, bye." Her head disappeared through her gate, and its portal snapped shut.

"What in the realms was that?" said Via, sputtering.

"I have no idea," said Fynne, looking concerned as he brushed himself off.

Grayson quickly brushed his hands off and sat up next to me. He went to help me get up, but I noticed something lying next to him on the gate circle. Whatever it was, it must have fallen out of his pocket. I gasped, realizing what it was.

"What's wrong, Wren?" Grayson followed my gaze. There, on the ground, was a dark stone. Grayson's eyes went wide. He quickly snatched it up and shoved it into his pocket. He then shot a glance at Via and Fynne, who had both stood up and were preoccupied with brushing themselves off. His eyes locked back on mine. They seemed to be pleading with me not to say anything. He then quickly stood up and held his hand out to me to help me up. I just lay there, staring at him, not sure if I should take it.

"Wren, please," he practically whispered, jerking his hand closer to me. I went to take his hand but stopped once again. In the middle of his hand, there was what looked like the exact same scar I now had on the back of my neck. Panicking even more, I pushed myself away back towards Via. Grayson looked confused and frustratedly looked at his hand.

"What is wrong-" he started to say but cut himself off, eyes once again going wide, and he quickly shoved his hand back into his pocket.

My mind was racing, going over every scenario of why Grayson would have a dark stone and the same exact scar as I did on his hand. I vaguely remember saying goodbye to Fynne, and Via who headed back into their realms then wondered why I wasn't telling them to stay. Grayson was clearly dangerous. Or was he? Kygra's words of his heart's soul also seemed to be playing over and over in the background of my thoughts. Before

I could even bring myself to say anything, Grayson and I were the only ones standing in the gate circle staring at each other. I felt out of breath.

I slowly started to back away from him towards my gate, thinking I could jump in my realm and close it if anything bad happened.

"Wren," said Grayson, stepping towards me. "I can explain."

"Stay right there!" I yelled, snapping out of my fog and into sharp reality. I held out my hand, ready to shoot a fireball if needed. Grayson stopped and held up his hands.

"Wren, I would never ever hurt you." He said with more sincerity than I thought him capable of.

"How would I know?" I said, now on the verge of tears. "You clearly have things you've hidden from me, so I have no reason whatsoever to trust you."

Grayson sighed. "You are right. But I did mean to tell you. This is just not how I pictured it happening."

"Tell me what?" I said, exasperated, "That you work for gate eleven? That you are a traitor?"

"Wren, no!"

"Then what? What is it?"

"Can I just show you?" He nodded towards his gateway.

"What? Your realm?"

"Yes," He said, walking up to me. "It will explain everything."

I looked at him skeptically. I mean, I really did want to see what was in his realm.

"Don't worry, it's completely safe, I promise." He looked so earnest I found myself nodding my head yes. Regardless of all the red flags, my curiosity was winning this one.

"Really?" He said as a quick smile spread across his face. "Great! Then, uh, let's go."

I let him grab my hand and lead me across the gate circle to his gate. He opened it and went to go through, but I paused. It was crazy to think that I was about to actually step through to the mysterious realm of The Chasm. I didn't feel mentally prepared for this at all.

"You ok?" he said, looking concerned.

"What? Oh, yes." I said nervously.

He grinned and ducked through the gate, his hand guiding me through after him.

I instantly felt dumb for not knowing what to expect. There was a deep chasm that stretched for what seemed like miles in front of me. Everything was charred black, and some places were smoking. Even the sky was a dark grayish color. I felt like Frodo, about to cross Mordor to drop the ring into Mount Doom. But instead of a volcano in the distance, I noticed a small piece of land that looked untouched and was full of beautiful trees and flowers. I stood there for a moment, taking it all in.

"What do you think?" asked Grayson nervously.

"Well, I can see why you call it The Chasm," I said.

Grayson chuckled. His odd happiness was contagious.

"Ya, I am not really creative when it comes to naming things." He said, "Its original name was Alure, but I didn't think it suited it, so I started calling it The Chasm."

"Alure?"

"Yes, this actually used to be Linore's personal realm that she and her lover called home."

My mind was blown.

"Well, you would think the person who had unlimited creative power would create something a little more, I don't know, homie?" I said looking around.

Grayson laughed again. I loved it.

"Well, it wasn't always like this. The little patch of paradise at the end of the chasm is what it was like. The rest was destroyed long ago, right before Linore disappeared."

"So, is it like a tropical realm?"

"Not exactly," Grayson said. "More like a creative realm. You can make it whatever you want. You want a sunset, I can make a sunset. You want a waterfall, I can make a waterfall. All of which I can still do on The Haven." He said, gesturing down the chasm.

My ears perked hearing my last name, Havyn. I went to say something about it but he continued.

"Unfortunately, the landscape around it is permanently charred and can't be manipulated anymore, except I can still make things appear, like this." He waved his hand, and the gate circle table materialized in front of us. It all started making sense.

"So, are you the only one here?" I asked, glancing around.

"Yes, just me."

"Then why not let anyone in and keep it such a guarded secret?"

He turned around and pointed to his gate. It was charred like everything else, but I noticed that more of the dark stones were embedded into the gate. I gasped and slowly backed away.

"Why are these here? And how did those other people from gate eleven get the stones they had?" I started panicking. "Are you giving these to them?"

"Wren, no, these have always been here. My whole job is to protect them. I have never given any of them away. The stones that the attackers had come from gate eleven."

I skeptically looked at him.

"Ok, if you look at the gate, there are five smaller dark stones and one larger one. I also keep this dark stone with me." He pulled out the stone he had dropped earlier from his pocket. "That makes seven dark stones that are under my protection. There are twelve dark stones in total, meaning that the other five must be in realm eleven."

I paused to think. "But why is one bigger?"

"Because it's the heart of the dark stone." He must have noticed the look of utter confusion on my face. "Ok, there is a lot to explain, so you will just have to bear with me. You ready?" He asked.

I nodded my head.

"Alright, so when Linore originally came through gate twelve she brought with her the Gemstone of Light, a stone containing the core of all magic. To create the realms, she split that stone into the twelve pieces, each one used to power each of the realms. Hence our gatekeeper stones," He tapped his own gatekeeper's stone. "The twelfth stone she kept for herself, which is known as the heart of the light stone. It is bigger than the rest. You got all that so far?" I nodded my head. "Ok, now the real world also contains its own stone. That is the core of what I imagine to be the absence of magic, and that stone is known as the dark stone. It used to be all one piece just like the light stone. One day, when Linore was here in The Chasm, someone broke in and attacked her with the dark stone. But when the intruder used his complete dark stone against just the heart of the light stone, the dark stone sensed the imbalance, so instead of attacking Linore, it rebounded and split itself into twelve pieces. That attempted attack is what caused the chasm you see here and the reason why these stones are embedded in my gate. So this bigger black stone is the heart of the dark stone."

"Then what exactly do they do? Do they have some sort of power?"

"That is a good question," said Grayson scratching his head. "So far, I have figured out that these stones are basically the exact opposite of magic. Anti-magic, if you will. I have also figured out that each of the dark stones seems to specifically combat its own realm, just like our gatekeeper stones control a specific realm. That's why we have these marks." He showed me the mark on his hand again. Just like my scar, there was a perfectly straight line down his palm, one half covered in the nasty half-circle scar and the other half completely smooth and untouched. I raised my hand behind my head and ran my fingers over my own mark. It felt much smoother than his scar looked.

"So you have your realm's dark stone then?" I asked.

"Yes," said Grayson, pulling out the dark stone from his pocket. "Only the dark stone to your realm can cause the marks. I have experimented with the other stones, and they don't cause the mark or the feeling of your soul splitting, but they still lessen your magic abilities quite a bit."

"So, what you are saying is that the person who attacked me was using the fantasy realm's dark stone against me?"

"That is correct," He responded. "That's good to know, it helps us to know what we are up against. Since they have the dark stone to your realm, we now know that you need to be especially guarded after."

He smiled at me and my heart jumped.

"I also know that they have the dark stone of the

mermaid realm, which Trez now has in his possession."

"So the reason why you asked Trez to keep it yourself was to protect it like the other stones?"

"Wait, how did you know that I asked for the dark stone?"

"Isla told me," I said nervously.

"Hmm..." he said, "Yes, that is why I wanted to take it. But I didn't explain why. I didn't want to let everyone know that I have these stones, they might have labeled me a 'bad guy' as well."

"Well, you being all secretive made us think that anyway," I said, rolling my eyes and laughing. He clearly didn't think it was funny. "I'm sorry, all I meant by that is that if you were a little bit more open about everything, everyone might think better of you and not be so suspicious. For example, why did you even hide that you knew Kygra was the gatekeeper to realm five? You could have just told us and totally avoided Root attacking you!"

"I wasn't sure!" he said. "And I didn't want to get your hopes up if it wasn't true."

"But you could have just said that!" I said. "If you did, the whole situation would have gone a lot smoother."

"But it did go smooth. It all worked out, right?" he said, glancing at me.

I glared at him.

"Alright, I guess I see your point." he sighed. "I am just

not used to being open with people, ok? I grew up my whole life keeping secrets, and life just seemed easier because of it."

"Well, now you have all of us gatekeepers!" I said, "And if you opened up to them like you just opened up to me, I am sure they will understand. They are all amazing people, and you are clearly on our side. You really have nothing to worry about."

Grayson sighed and scratched his head. "I'll think about it," He finally said.

I crossed my arms and groaned.

"Common Wren, it's not that easy. I just told you I am not used to this," he whined.

"But it will be easier if you just start sharing your secrets!"

"Speaking of secrets, I have another one for you," he said, taking a step towards me and leaning in close to my ear. I stood there frozen, his warm breath brushing my cheek.

"I really... " he whispered slowly, then paused.

"Yes?" I asked intently. My heart was pounding so loudly at this point I was sure he could hear it.

"...want to show you the rest of my realm." he finished quickly. He then spun around and took off, running down the chasm before I could say anything. I also could have sworn I heard him chuckling to himself as he went. I couldn't tell what I was more upset with, the fact that he changed the subject or the fact I fell for it.

The Haven, as Grayson called it, was on a perfect circle

of untouched wonderland. I found it even more enchanting than Fairy Glenn in my realm, which was saying a lot. It stood slightly above the rest of the charred earth, so Grayson had to help me up onto it. As soon as my feet landed on the soft grass, the air smelled like the candle store at our local mall, a million different scents at once but all melding into one that smelled absolutely amazing.

"Amazing, isn't it?" He said smiling. "When Linore was attacked, the heart of the light stone protected her with a dome of magic. That dome also preserved the area around her, which is what you see here." He ran up to a nearby tree. "What's your favorite fruit?" He asked, turning back to me.

"Umm, peach."

Grayson lifted his hand up just as a peach grew from the tree. By the time his hand reached it, it was full-grown, and he plucked it off the tree. He turned around and handed it to me.

"Impressive, is it not?" He said, imitating Via's ridiculous meeting accent.

"Tis quite the spectacle," I said, mimicking the same accent.

Grayson smirked. I took a bite. It was the best tasting peach I had ever eaten in my life.

"Oh my goodness, this is incredible," I said, taking another bite.

"I knew you would love it."

He continued to show me around The Haven, which

didn't take long because it was contained in about a 50-foot circle. He showed me where he would create a hammock to sleep in when staying there and how he would then turn the sky into the most beautiful star-filled galaxy to help him fall asleep. Even though everything was so beautiful, I couldn't help but stare at him. It felt so good to see him smiling. He was clearly excited to be showing me around, but the more I watched him, the more I could sense a hint of sadness behind his shining eyes. Eventually, we sat down near the little pond in the center of the haven. The sky was still filled with stars, and I could hear crickets chirping along with the gurgling pond. Grayson laid back in the grass next to me and let out a long contented sigh.

"You have no idea how great it is to finally show you my realm," he said.

"What kept you from letting me in before?" I asked.

"My mom had warned me not to ever, under any circumstance, let anyone in."

"Your mom?" I asked.

"Oh, uh, yes, she was the last gatekeeper. Just like your realm, our stone is handed down through the generations."

"Right, I remember you telling me that," I said. "Then where is she now? Does she come back to visit at all?"

"She's dead," he said simply.

"Oh, I'm sorry."

"It happened about 5 years ago now," continued Grayson. "Jumana was actually the one who found her and tracked me down in the real world to tell me. I was devastated. My mom and I were very close. We spent a lot of time here, which my dad hated. So when she passed, my dad became even more bitter towards it all. But coming here is all I had left of mom, so despite his protests, I kept coming… " he trailed off, deep in memories. "Sorry, I didn't mean for that to get so dark," he said, suddenly sitting all the way up.

"No, no, it's totally fine," I said. "I really appreciate you telling me. It helps me to understand you more, and it's good practice for you to be more open." I smiled at him.

Grayson blushed.

Without warning, he abruptly stood up. "Well, are you ready to get back?" He held out both his hands to me to help me up.

To be honest, I wasn't ready and wanted to stay here forever, but I grabbed his hands and let him pull me up. I wasn't prepared for his strength and tight grip, and I ended up falling forward into him. I stayed there, my hands and head resting on his chest. I could feel his heart pounding. Grayson waited a moment, his hands down by his side. He then abruptly wrapped me in a tight hug. I reached around his torso and hugged him back. I was suddenly so relieved. I hadn't realized just how bad I wanted him to be good, to be someone I could trust. I never wanted to let go. Suddenly Grayson stepped back.

"I uh, should probably get you back home now," he said, clearing his throat.

"Oh yes, that would be good," I said, feeling embarrassed. The trust I thought we had gained seemed distant once again, like we left off right where we started.

"Alright then, shall we?" he said, taking off down the chasm. He was walking so fast I was practically running to catch up.

※

We made it back to the gate, and Grayson went through without even looking back at me. I followed, feeling foolish for letting him play with my emotions like this. How could he be so caring one moment and so distant the next? As I emerged out of the gate, I felt Grayson's arm stop me from stepping any further. I looked up at him, his face dead set on whatever was in front of us. I followed his gaze. There, in the middle of the gate circle, sitting on the gate key pedestal, was a young man who looked to be just a little bit older than Grayson and me. He had neat, light brown hair and was wearing a fancy long coat trimmed with gold. There was also a woman with him who was leaning against the pedestal next to him. She was wearing mostly black and had a head covering so that just her face was visible.

"Ah, Grayson," said the man, "Just the man I wanted to see. I haven't heard from you in a while, I just wanted to see if you have thought any more about my offer?"

Chapter
16

"Grayson, who is this?" I nervously whispered.

Grayson didn't say anything but quickly reached over and closed his gate.

"Ah, I see we have a guest, my apologies for not introducing myself," said the man as he hopped off the pedestal. He smiled, which looked odd and deformed. As he came closer, I realized it was because of a long scar running down his face.

"My name is Ryker, gatekeeper of the eleventh realm. I am surprised Grayson here hasn't told you about me. What a shame." He walked towards us. Grayson stepped in front of me.

"Ah, I see how it is," said Ryker, coming to a stop. I suddenly heard Grayson's voice in my head. He was sending a message to Launch, Fynne, and Trez to come to the gate circle. He must have included me to let me know what was going on. The girl with Ryker flinched. She slowly walked up behind Ryker and touched his shoulder. After a brief pause, Ryker continued. "I see you have warned the others about us being here, so I am going to make this quick."

I looked at Grayson to see his reaction to this, but he just kept staring at them.

"My offer still stands, you give me the heart of the dark stone, and in return, I will tell you where Linore is."

I gasped. "You know where Linore is?" I took a step towards him, but Grayson once again held me back.

Ryker laughed. "As a matter of fact, I do, I just can't get to her, but you definitely could."

"We can't trust him," Grayson muttered.

The thought of permanently fixing the crisis in my realm was enticing. "But I thought we needed to collect all the gatekeeper stones in order to summon her?"

"Whoever said that?" asked Ryker mockingly. "And once you got all the stones together how would you even summon her?"

I felt embarrassed. I hadn't really even thought that far. I just thought that if they were all together, it would just... you know... happen. I slowly realized I might have been just making up things that sounded good.

Ryker continued, "Besides, a little birdy told me you have found the gatekeeper's stone to gate five, the animal realm, correct?"

I didn't respond.

"I'll take your silence as a yes," he smirked. "In that case, that only leaves realm nine. And what if I told you I knew where that one was as well?"

I looked over at Grayson, who was still staring at Ryker intently.

"But that is beside the point. The main thing is finding Linore, right? Oh, and by the way, how is your realm, Wren?" He said, stepping closer and reaching out to touch my face. "Peaceful, I hope?"

"That's enough," growled Grayson as he swatted Ryker's hand away. "We can't give you the heart of the dark stone. That's final. However, finding Linore would be beneficial. I propose a different exchange. We can give you back your minion."

Ryker laughed so obnoxiously it made me angry. "Who, Ava? Why would I want her back? Besides, she went directly against my orders. She deserves to rot in whatever prison you're keeping her in."

"Well, if there can be no arrangement, then we are at an impasse," said Grayson in a light British accent.

"This is no time to be quoting movies," I hissed at Grayson.

"Ah, but Grayson, when you look at all of this, we essentially want the same thing." Ryker sat back on the pedestal. "Face it. You want to erase magic just as much as I do."

"What?" I said, taking a step back from Grayson.

Grayson just stood there silently, glaring at Ryker.

"Wait, you haven't told her that yet either?" Ryker laughed once again.

Fynne's gate came to life at that moment, and he stepped out in his full armor, sword drawn.

"Ah yes," said Ryker, hopping off the pedestal once again. "Perfect timing, Mi, go ahead."

Suddenly the girl in black bounded across the gate circle. Just as Fynne was about to swing his sword at her, she launched herself in the air, flipping so that she landed behind him but facing his direction. She touched his shoulder, and he instantaneously stopped trying to attack her. He turned around to face her, taking off his chest plate of armor as he did. The armor clattered to the floor, and he began to fumble with his gatekeeper's stone that was strapped to his chest.

"Fynne, no!" Yelled Grayson, taking a step towards him.

Ryker advanced towards us. "Careful, Grayson," He sneered. "You leave, and I get your lady."

Grayson quickly jumped back in front of me. The air around us felt like it was sizzling, and my hair was standing on end. Grayson's arms flew back behind him, almost wrapping around me. Then, he thrust both hands forward again and lightning burst from them, sending Ryker flying back directly into the stone archway of his gate. The force was so incredible I thought for sure Ryker was dead. However, he quickly composed himself and got back on his feet.

"Interesting," he said, eyebrows raised. "Your power is quite impressive, unlike any I have seen." He walked back towards us. "But it's still useless, you know, you will never win."

I ducked behind Grayson, who was clearly far more skilled than me in fighting and shot a glance towards Fynne. He still had his gatekeeper's stone in one hand, and the girl was now placing a dark stone in his other hand. I panicked. I was sure she was trying to kill him by splitting his soul. Without even thinking, I created a fireball in my hand but hesitated to throw it. I didn't want to hit Fynne.

Right then, Launch burst through his realm.

"Launch, Fynne!" I yelled at the top of my lungs.

Launch glanced to where I was pointing and took off in a dead sprint. He held out his hand towards the girl and jerked it towards where Grayson and I were standing. She suddenly went flying through the air and slammed into gate seven. Unlike Ryker, she didn't get up right away. Ryker stopped walking towards us, distracted by his sidekick.

"Fynne No!" yelled Launch. A loud boom echoed through the gate circle and left my ears ringing. Fynne was now holding the two stones together, the flat sides facing each other. The stones started to glow intensely, burning Fynne's hands. This woke Fynne from whatever trance he was in, and he quickly dropped them, screaming in agony. When the gems hit the ground, they didn't split but stayed melded together. The screaming continued as Fynne's gate went completely dark.

"What did you do?!" Grayson yelled at Ryker.

"What did I do? You mean what did you do! It didn't have to come to this, you know. We could have worked things out quite nicely if you had just given me the heart of the dark stone. And now the only way to clean up this little mess you created is to find Linore, so I suggest you start rethinking your answer."

The limp body of his sidekick began to stir, and she slowly stood up just as Gate eight sprang to life.

Trez jumped out of his gate and took in the scene, first looking to the girl struggling to stand at the gate next to him, then to Grayson and I, then to Fynne and Launch, and then lastly on Ryker.

"You!" He roared.

"And that, my friends, is my cue to leave. Mi, pick it up. We have to go," Ryker said as he quickly turned around to face his gate. Mi groaned. "Hey, you!" she yelled at me. I looked over. "Tell J I said hi, will you?" she smirked as she tapped her knuckles on gate seven. She popped something into her mouth and bit down on it. She instantly stood up straight and bounded after Ryker, tumbling and performing several flips and twists, as if nothing had happened. Her unnatural speed got her to the gate just as Ryker opened it, and she gracefully jumped through.

Ryker paused before going in. "You know how to reach me." He said, looking at Grayson and pointing to his head, "I'll be waiting." He disappeared through the gate.

Trez, who had taken off running towards Ryker, let out one last scream as he launched himself towards the fading gate. But instead of disappearing like Ryker, he crashed into the forest beyond, the sound of snapping twigs and crashing bushes echoing through the circle. "No!" He cried, "No, no, no!" He was pounding the ground and sobbing. I looked over at Fynne, who had pushed Launch aside and was scrambling back towards his own gate. He had picked up the two fused stones and was frantically trying to open his own gate, but to no avail.

"What did she do!?" He screamed. "My family is in there!" He sobbed "My family!"

Tears welled up in my eyes. Grayson was breathing heavily in front of me.

"Grayson?" I said.

"What, Wren?" he snapped.

I backed away, not sure I could handle one more thing going wrong.

"Wren, I am sorry, that was harsh." He grabbed his head. "This is not how I thought this would all go down. This isn't what I wanted."

I had nothing to say. I couldn't. Grayson looked up and reached out to me.

"Wren, I..." I backed away, my mind racing. I felt like my trust in Grayson was swinging on a pendulum. Right now, it was smack in the middle.

Grayson withdrew his hand, looking even more hurt.

He suddenly stood up and took off running through the woods. I didn't do anything to stop him.

Chapter
17

"Would you like some more tea?" asked Jumana as she reached across the table to grab the teapot.

"Yes, please." I held out my cup for her to refill, and I reclined back into the mound of ornate pillows that surrounded the low table we sat at. A cool breeze caused the sheer curtains that surrounded us on her veranda to flutter gently, and I briefly closed my eyes to take it all in. Jumana had just quietly listened to me sharing all the details of what happened a few days before, only interrupting once to ask about the girl Ryker called Ti or Mi or whatever. It felt good to get it all off my chest.

"Well, that is quite the story," said Jumana as she sat back in her seat across from me. "Now that you have told me everything, what are your thoughts on it?"

I sighed. "I don't know," I adjusted my position in the

pillows. "I don't feel like my brain can handle this all. I am just overwhelmed."

"About what?" said Jumana

"Everything!" I said, "The fact that Fynne can't see his family and we have no clue how to fix it other than finding Linore, which the only way we can is to give the heart of all non-magic to a guy who seems to be willing to do anything to eradicate magic which Grayson seems to be on board with!"

"Have you tried talking to Grayson?" asked Jumana.

"Yes!" I said, "I have texted him multiple times, but he hasn't responded."

"Well, what if he is not sure what he thinks right now, just like you. And he needs some time to sort it out."

I took a moment to ponder this. "That is a good point I guess,"

"I think you need to start seeing this situation from his point of view. Grayson has been through a lot."

"Yes, true," I said as I slowly traced the rim of my teacup with my finger. "He told me about his mother."

"Oh really," said Jumana. "What did he say?"

"He said that she died in the gate circle and you were the one that found her. He also said you tracked him down in the real world to tell him."

"Yes, that is true," she said, sipping her tea. "And maybe that has something to do with the fact he wants to get rid of magic. Have you thought about that?"

"You think so?" I asked, "So it was magic that got her killed?"

"That is what it appeared to be," said Jumana, looking off into the distance.

"I mean, I guess if magic was the reason one of my parents died, I would hate it too. But at the same time, magic is also amazing. And maybe it was just an accident." I paused and vigorously stirred my tea with my spoon. "Do you think magic should go away?"

"Wren, I have seen a lot of things in my days here." She said, setting down her tea. "And I have come to find that the less magic there is, the more room there is for love."

"What do you mean?" I asked, confused.

"For example," she continued, "Grayson's magic can enable him to create things out of thin air, correct?"

"Umm, yes," I said.

"So say he wanted to give you a present," she continued. "Which present would you appreciate more, one that he made appear out of thin air or one that he spent time making and putting thought into?"

"Well, the second one, I guess," I said.

"Exactly," said Jumana. "Or let's say you had the option of teleporting somewhere as Launch can in his realm. Sure, it can be convenient but think of all the new things you could learn about the person you are with if you spent time traveling the normal way."

I pondered this for a moment. "So, you do want to get rid of magic?"

"To some extent, I already have, at least here in my own realm," she said. "Years ago, I decreed that all Gemstones of Light be collected and locked up, you know, the small clear stones that give the wearer greater magical abilities."

I nodded.

"Well, the abilities that these stones provided were too powerful, and people abused it greatly. After watching for years the destruction and discord it caused amongst my people I decided it wasn't a power people should possess, so I had them rounded up and locked away. Even though it brought much peace, that decision did end up costing me greatly..." She trailed off, deep within her own thoughts. "So I know what's right, but I am also afraid of the changes it will bring. In some ways, I can understand Grayson's struggle. So I really don't have an answer for you. But what I can say is this. Whatever you all decide to do, I will always have your backs. You are all good kids, and I know you will make the right decision."

I sighed and sunk further into the pillows.

"I know it's a lot to think about," said Jumana. "Let's narrow it down. What can you do at this exact moment to help the situation?"

I took a moment to think "Probably to just wait for Grayson to be ready to talk, he is really the only one that can do something at this point."

"Good," said Jumana. "Sounds like a plan. Communication is always key."

"I should also check on my realm," I continued, "I have been so preoccupied with everything I never checked in with Falveron on how things were going last time we were there."

"Even better," said Jumana. "And don't worry, I think Grayson will be ready to talk to you sooner than you think."

She poured herself some more tea.

"So Grayson," she said smiling, "He is pretty nice, huh?"

"Jumana!"

"What?" she laughed. "Come on, don't tell me you don't like him."

No matter how hard I tried, I couldn't hide my smile.

"Oh, fine," I said. "Maybe I like him just a little bit."

"Just a little bit?" scoffed Jumana. "Seems to me you think more of him than that."

"To be honest, I am not sure what I think," I said, reaching for another sugar cube. "I have been so back and forth on how I feel about him, or even if I trust him."

"Well, if it helps you at all, I believe he has a heart of gold, and I completely approve," she said. "He just has to sort out a few things, that's all. Sounds like you need to do the same too. I really think you both could help each other out in more ways than you think."

"You know what I think?" I said.

"What?"

"That it's time for me to check on my realm," I said, standing up.

Jumana laughed. "Alright, I am done. I've probably said too much already."

Jumana's words played through my head as we made it back to her gate. It was nice to be reassured that Grayson was good, especially coming from Jumana and not a crazy-haired dragon lady babbling on about heart soul stuff. But I did wish that it wasn't so awkward sometimes when Grayson and I tried to communicate. Why couldn't he be more like Root? I always felt comfortable around Root. Our conversations were so easy and carefree. He represented stability and safety in my life, two things I really needed right now.

༺✿༻

I practically ran across the gate circle to my realm, feeling really excited to see Root and give him a big hug. Jumana watched from her gate to make sure I was ok. I waved back at her and ducked into mine.

I took a piece of paper out of my satchel and started scribbling out a note to send to Root, letting him know I was here. I knew he would be upset if I walked into town again without him. I quickly finished and walked to the edge of the plateau to send it. I watched it float down towards Luma which was on fire.

Chapter 18

I took off running down the steep path into town, hoping this was just a random fire, but due to the number of scattered buildings on fire, I knew this must be some kind of attack. I scolded myself for not asking Falveron when I was here last. I shouldn't have assumed that a couple of working gemstones could solve this problem. At any rate, this was not something I was prepared to deal with.

As I got closer, I realized the fire was coming from the northwest quarter of the city, primarily where the elves lived. I tried stopping people running away in the streets to see if they could tell me what was going on but received no clear reply. The panic was palpable.

I finally turned the last corner and immediately closed my eyes, the raging fire from the first building stinging them.

I took a moment to back up and blink my eyes open. Utter chaos came into view. Dwarves, humans, and elves, mixed with the castle soldiers, were all fighting in the streets. I started to panic. This was far worse than I could have imagined. I mustered what strength I could and ran towards the inferno in front of me. I figured I could use the fire quenching technique Root taught me. I was just about to raise my hands to perform it when I was abruptly stopped by an arm slamming into my chest and scooping me up. I jerked my head up, thinking it was Root, but realized it was Captain Tarren. He grabbed my hand and ran in the opposite direction, barking orders to the surrounding soldiers. Two soldiers broke off and followed us as we ran through the streets. The commotion slowly faded and the streets became deserted. We finally stopped in an alley and Captain Tarren ordered the soldiers to stand guard at either end. He turned back to me and grabbed my shoulders.

"What on earth were you doing? Are you hurt?" He turned me around, checking my arms and legs.

"No, no, I am fine," I stuttered. "I just thought I could help. Root taught me how to put out fires and-"

"Wren," said the captain, "You cannot just run into a battle, especially as the gatekeeper! What if someone got a hold of your gatekeeper stone? That could have been disastrous!" He turned from me in frustration. My emotions got the better of me, and I burst into tears.

"I am so sorry, Wren," He said calmly, turning back

to me. "Things have taken a nasty turn, and we aren't able to control it."

"Control what?" I sobbed, "What is going on? No one would tell me anything."

Captain Tarren sighed. "From what I understand, the dwarves snuck into the city and raided people's houses for more gate key gemstones. The people retaliated, and it escalated quickly." He rubbed his temples. He was clearly exhausted. "On top of that, Root..."

"Root what?" I asked, snapping my head up to look him in the face.

The captain shook his head.

"What happened? Tell me!" I was screaming at this point.

"Root was gravely injured. A dwarf jumped him and he wasn't able to dodge the-" He stopped mid-sentence and glanced at me. "Anyway, he was still alive when they took him away." He started pacing instead of continuing. My heart stopped, but my mind started racing.

"Where is he?" I yelled again.

"He should be back at the castle," said Tarren. "And that is where I am taking you. So if you are good, we should get going right away." He signaled the soldiers to come back. Tarren started to guide me out of the alley.

"Wait!" I yelled, "I may have something in my apothecary shop that could possibly help! It's just down the street here." The soldiers stopped and looked at Tarren for orders. I didn't wait and took off running. Three blocks later, I found myself at my shop, a closed sign hanging in the window. I banged on the door. "Milly! Are in there! It's me, Wren!" I remembered I wore the key to the shop around my neck. I fumbled to get it off when the door burst open, the shop bell ringing loudly. A frightened Milly stood panting in the doorway.

"Are you ok?" I asked, wrapping her in a hug

"I am fine," she said, clinging to me. "I was just closing shop. I hope you are not mad! I was just scared."

"Oh, Milly, I am not mad at all! You did the right thing!" I let go of her and ran towards the back of the shop. She followed, "we are headed to the castle now, and you are coming with us to be safe. I just need to find the health potions I was working on. Root is hurt." The shop bell rang again.

"Wren, where are you?" came the captain's voice.

"Back here!" I yelled as I stuffed one of my bags full of the little potion jars.

"Wait, this new apothecary shop is yours?" asked Tarren, trying to figure out where my voice was coming from. "Yes," I yelled. "That is a story for a different time." I popped my head to the front and signaled him and the soldiers to follow me. "We can go out the back. It's quicker."

Milly locked the front door, and we all made our way to the back alley. The commotion sounded closer now. We took off running, Tarren, Milly, and I all together with one soldier in front of us and one soldier behind. We only had to reroute once because we came across another part of the fight, but we made it back to the castle in one piece. The large gates to the castle's courtyard that had always been open as long as I had been here were now barred shut. Tarren directed us to a secret entrance where he announced our arrival. The door immediately swung in, and we were ushered in. The courtyard was all a bustle. Soldiers were everywhere, horses were being saddled, and injured were being tended to.

"Captain Tarren!" Falveron emerged and came towards us.

"Where is Root?" I shouted, running towards him.

"Inside, the first door on the left," he said, pointing towards the castle entrance. I took off immediately.

I knew exactly what room it was. It was the room Root had pulled me in before we left the last time I was there. I ran through the open door and stopped in my tracks. There was Root, laying in a bed they had set up for him, his face pale and gray. I gasped and grabbed the door frame for support. There were several nurses in the room helping him, one of them being my maid Lyra.

"Is he..." I trailed off.

"He is still with us," said Lyra, moving out of the way so I could stand beside him.

I walked over, now being able to see what happened

to him. He had a large gash on his left shoulder. It looked as if someone had tried to hack his arm off.

"He has lost a lot of blood," said Lyra, putting her hand on my shoulder. "We have tried everything, but unfortunately, our realms' powers aren't strong when it comes to healing."

This I knew very well because even experimenting with healing potions had yielded very weak results. Regardless, I opened my bag and started sorting through all the potions I had dumped in my bag. I started giving him everything I thought might help. I was so frantic I almost gave him an invisibility potion which would have made things even worse. I finally got to the bottom of my bag, but the wound looked no better. I then tried using my gatekeeper stone, but no matter how much I searched the shelves in my mind, I couldn't find anything to heal him. With all the magic in this realm, you'd think there would be something that would help, but no, we were limited to fireballs and housekeeping tricks. Frustrated, I threw my now emptied bag down and started to pace the room, trying to rack my brain for any sort of solution.

The nurses went back to tending him, saying that the bleeding actually slowed down a little bit which was good. But one look at his face still told me there wasn't much time.

"Come on Wren, think!" I muttered under my breath. Maybe someone else had healing powers? But who? Launch? He was always coming up with crazy things with his stone. Maybe he could heal? Or maybe Jumana? She had wisdom, but her realm seemed pretty laid back. Maybe healing was a part of that? Nothing sounded right, though. I rubbed my neck in frustration. As I did, my hand brushed over the top of my scar.

"Trez!" I yelled out loud. Everyone in the room suddenly looked at me. "Sorry," I whispered. I quickly stepped out of the room. Via had said that Trez was the one that gave her the salve that had healed the injury on my neck, and even Grayson marveled at how well it worked. I quickly sent Trez a message asking if he had anything else that could heal Root. He responded within the minute.

"Sounds pretty bad, but yes, I do have something that will definitely help. I just need to get more of it. Unfortunately, it's in a place I don't necessarily want to be seen, but I could figure it out."

My eyes shifted to the invisibility potion on the floor where I had tossed it after almost giving it to Root. I snatched it up and ran out of the castle.

"Someone get me a horse!" I yelled.

Chapter 19

The smell of sea salt and the sound of ocean waves greeted me as Trez guided me through his gate and into his realm. Trez's gate was the mouth of Skull Rock, a rock shaped like, you guessed it, a skull. It was located in the corner of a small cove where Trez's ship was currently anchored. The cove itself was nestled at the bottom of steep cliffs, but one path led up into the town above, which was one of the only neutral areas in Trez's realm. That meant no one was allowed to attack each other there. The pirates here were pretty ruthless.

Riggs, Trez's right-hand man, was there to meet us. He was very tall and muscular, had dark skin, and an eye patch over his right eye. He looked very intimidating, but there was a peace about him that could calm a crying baby. Even though I had only met him a few times, he still came up to me and wrapped me in a big hug.

"Wren!" He exclaimed. "I am so sorry to hear about your realm and your friend. Hopefully Trez here can get the antidote quickly and you'll be back in no time."

"Thanks, Riggs," I replied.

"Yes, the sooner we get this done, the better," said Trez, quickly walking down the beach towards the dinghy that would get us back to his ship. He frustratedly tugged at the anchor, threw it in the boat, then kicked it back into the water. I looked at Riggs, who patted my shoulder to let me know it was ok. Whatever happened in the gate circle the other day must really be taking a toll on Trez for him to be acting like this. We got into the Dinghy and headed back to the ship. I wanted to know if he was doing okay but felt it wasn't the time.

"How is Fynne doing?" I asked instead.

"He is in Sylum," said Trez gesturing to the town in the distance. "After we got back, we tried everything to separate the two stones, but nothing worked. We also tried contacting Grayson, but there has been no response."

"Same," I said.

"That kid better get it together soon. Fynne is losing it. Not to mention I am pretty upset myself. I get that he is processing all this like we all are, but he should at least be talking to us about it!" said Trez, slamming his fist on the side of the boat. Riggs caught my attention and shook his head, and I didn't bring the subject up again.

We made it back to the ship, and Trez started barking orders. By the time he made it to the helm, the sails were opened, and the men were standing at attention waiting for the next orders.

"Wren, come over here and grab ahold of this railing. You'll need the support," said Riggs.

"For what?" I asked. There was no time for a response because as soon as Trez's hands touched the wheel, the sails billowed, and the ship took off like a shot. I almost became very closely acquainted with the ship's deck, but thank goodness Riggs jumped towards me and caught me in time. He laughed.

"A perk of being the gatekeeper here." He smiled.

I brushed myself off. I had been to the pirate realm a few times before but had never been on Trez's ship. The wind whipping around my face and through my hair felt so good. I took a deep breath, glad for a brief moment to be free from all my current worries, which quickly came flooding back.

"So," I said, turning back to Riggs, "Where is this antidote? I don't even know what it is."

"It's a plant on Bliss," said Riggs. He saw my confused face and continued. "It's an island that Trez used to visit frequently. The antidote is a flower that turns from white to purple in the sunlight. It is most potent when it's purple."

"Used too?" I asked, "Does he not go there anymore?"

Riggs shook his head. "It was taken over by a buffoon of a pirate. Trez could have easily won it back, but he chose just to let it go."

"But why?" I pressed, "Especially since it has a plant like that on it."

"Well, we did have some stored up for a while but the last of it Trez used to help heal your wound."

"Oh, I am sorry," I said blushing.

"Oh Wren, don't worry yourself. Trez would do anything for the gatekeepers and he was very glad to help, just like he is now."

I nodded my thanks.

"That is not the main reason though." Riggs sighed. "Let's just say that the memories that were made on that island are now too painful for him." Riggs didn't continue and I didn't ask any further questions.

We sailed out of the cove and were making our way along the coast. Trez, at one point, came down and invited Riggs and me into the captain's quarters.

"Alright, we will be passing the island shortly," said Trez as soon as we were inside. "I am going to jump ship and swim to shore. Hopefully, Trigger and his gang are preoccupied. The last thing I want to do is start a fight."

"Oh wait," I said, opening my satchel. "I brought this for

you. It's an invisibility potion."

"Really?" said Trez. "How long does it last?"

"This is a half portion, so maybe half an hour?" I said.

"Perfect," He said as he abruptly popped to cork off and downed it. Moments later, he completely disappeared. "Thanks, Wren, this is great," I heard his voice say.

A satchel sitting next to his desk suddenly disappeared along with a few other items from his desk.

"Riggs, I set the ship to sail around Bandon Island and pass by this exact way again. Just be sure to have a rope ready on the starboard side, and I'll use that to come back aboard."

"You got it," said Riggs. I heard Trez patting Riggs on the shoulder, and then the cabin doors opened up. I exited the cabin, and sure enough, the tall cliffs of an island were on our left. Before I could even make it to the side of the boat to watch, I heard a splash, and Trez was gone.

The island was beautiful and covered with lush, tropical trees and plants. Even the cliffs were covered with different flowers and vines.

"Is he going to climb that cliff?" I asked Riggs, concerned if Trez was even going to make it.

"No," He replied. "You see that cave at the base of the cliff? That is how he will get to the flowers."

Movement at the top of the cliff caught my eye. It was some sort of lookout, and a few pirates stared down at our ship. None of them made a move, though. Riggs came and stood beside me, noticing what I was looking at.

"Good thing you brought that potion. This could have gotten messy."

We continued to sail on, the ship now steering itself. I took a seat at the ship's bow and watched as the crew members relaxed and sat around on boxes and piles of rope. Soon Riggs joined me.

"Riggs, it seems like Trez can run this ship on his own. If you don't mind me asking, why does he have a crew?"

Riggs stared off into the distance towards another island just coming into view. "You are right," he said. "He really doesn't need any of us."

"I'm sorry," I stammered. "I didn't mean it like that. I was just wondering-"

"No worries, Wren," He reassured me. "We all know that we aren't necessarily needed. It's more like we needed him. Every single one of us was abandoned as children, and Trez has helped us." He smiled. "You see, we are actually all children of the mermaid realm." My eyes widened.

"Hold up," I said. "So you are saying that you were all originally mermaids? Even Trez?!"

"Yes," laughed Riggs.

I immediately couldn't wait to tell Via this juicy information.

"So, what do you mean you were all abandoned?" I asked.

"Well, the problem with the mermaid realm is that there aren't enough mermaid gate key gemstones." I nodded, remembering what Isla said at our first meeting. "So whenever a royal is born, they start taking gemstones from the people, more specifically the male children. You see, it is considered a curse to have a boy in the mermaid realm unless, of course, you're a royal. In that case, it's a blessing. Anyway, the common people adore the royals so much that when they are asked to give up one of their family's gemstones, it's considered a high honor. So in a way, most of our parents joyfully let us go. They then bring us to the surface, take our stone and basically leave us to die." Riggs sighed and looked over at me, horror written all over my face. "I know, messed up, isn't it." He suddenly stood up. "Speaking of which, here is the island we were all left on." The ship had now reached the small island we saw off in the distance and started to make its way around it. The crew suddenly all got up and gathered on one side of the ship facing the island's shore. There was a little shack on one of the beaches.

"No flag today, sir!" Shouted one of the crewmates. His voice sounded so young, and when I got a closer look, I realized he couldn't have been more than twelve years old.

"Thanks, Kiff," said Riggs. The shack door on the shore opened, and an old woman hobbled out. She waved as we passed by, and all the crew members waved and shouted greetings.

He turned back to me and continued, "That is Diana.

She lives in that shack and keeps an eye out for any abandoned children. She raises a flag to signal us so we can take them aboard. Before Trez started taking kids in, she would bring them back to Sylum, the sanctuary town above the gate. That is how Trez and I met. I was abandoned first, and then a couple of days later, Trez was. She paired us up in Sylum, where we lived in the streets, scraping along. Trez was very driven and a great leader, even at the age of eleven. Kids seemed to be drawn to him and listened to him. He would always talk of his dream to one day becoming the gatekeeper, and the way he spoke about it made everyone believe he could do it..." Riggs trailed off, deep in old memories. "Anyway," he continued, "We would all gladly lay down our lives for him if the need presented itself. He has done so much for us and has given us a family."

A little later, Bliss Island came back into view, and Riggs grabbed a rope and made sure it was on the starboard side like Trez requested.

"Aren't you going to tie it to something and let it in the water so he can grab it?" I asked, looking confused at the pile of rope he had just set down and walked away from.

"Just watch," smiled Riggs.

We were directly in front of the island now, and the crew was searching the water for Trez. Riggs was just leaning on the main mast watching the pile of rope. Just as I thought that maybe Trez had missed us coming back, the rope sprang to life all on its own. One end dove down into the water, and the other flew up towards the rigging. The rope became taught and pulled up what I assumed was Trez. The end of the rope came into view over the side, and I heard a loud thump followed by a large puddle of water appearing on the deck. I watched as wet footprints led back to Trez's cabin. He became visible as he was reaching the cabin door. He motioned for Riggs and me to join him. Riggs made it to the cabin first, and I stopped just inside the door, wondering if they wanted it closed. They already seemed deep in a private conversation.

I suddenly heard Trez yell, "Essie would have been so upset!"

Riggs was clearly trying to calm a pacing Trez down. "I mean, the place was a mess. They even tore down our treehouse. I am glad they didn't find the flowers, or else we would all be in the middle of an all-out brawl."

"Remember, you are the one who let Trigger have it. It was your choice," said Riggs.

"I know, I know," said Trez, running his hands through his messy hair. They both stopped and suddenly looked up at me.

"Sorry Wren," said Trez, shaking his head. "This isn't your problem, my apologies. You can close the door and come on in. I was able to get the flowers for you." He opened his satchel and pulled out a small wooden box which he opened to reveal gorgeous pure white flowers. He also set down a jar. "I picked off all the flowers and then harvested the bulb which

I have in here." He said, tapping the jar, "I want you to bring it back to your realm and grow it there. It will be safer there. The only favor I ask is that I would be able to get healing potions from you whenever I need them"

"Of course!" I said, "And if you ever need any other potions, just let me know. It's the least I can do." I stuffed the flowers and the bulb into my bag.

Trez sighed and sat back in his chair.

༺༻

Moments later, we were back at the cove the gate was located in, and Riggs readied the dinghy for us to go ashore. As we headed back, I suddenly heard gunshots that echoed throughout the cove. I ducked my head and squealed, but Trez and Riggs sat there as if everything was completely fine.

"Sounds like Lias is back at it again," said Trez. Another gunshot sounded.

"He's fighting Mop's gang," Riggs said

"That'll be a quick fight," replied Trez.

"Mmmm," grunted Riggs.

I lifted my head, Riggs was picking out dirt from under his nails and Trez reclining in the bow.

"Is it always like this?" I asked nervously.

"This is nothing," said Trez. "The fighting is more subdued around Sylum. You get further out, and it's absolute cutthroat out there. And all for this," Trez patted his chest. He must strap his gatekeeper's stone to his chest just like Kygra and Fynne.

We reached the shore, and Trez opened the gate.

"Now remember, the flowers are most potent in the sunlight when it is at its deepest shade of purple. Drinking or eating them is the best, but you can also mash them up and turn them into a salve, like the one I gave Via for your injury. I am sure you can also make it stronger with whatever you do to make your other potions, so feel free to experiment. There is not much you can do to ruin it."

"Thanks again," I said, heading towards the open gate. Trez walked me back through to watch me walk to my gate. I almost stopped to ask him about Essie, because let's face it, I was curious, but it almost felt rude at this point to bring it up. I was halfway to my gate when gate six came to life, and Grayson walked out.

Chapter 20

Grayson immediately saw me and started walking towards me.

"Wren, I'm so sorry..." He trailed off and stopped walking as soon as he noticed Trez.

Trez, who was leaning on his gate, pushed himself off and started walking towards Grayson. His pace quickened as he went, and before I knew it, Trez's rope that he kept at his side leaped out and wrapped itself around Grayson's arms and torso. Grayson squirmed to get out and was just about to fall over when Trez caught him by the throat.

"Where in the blue blazes have you been?" growled Trez as he pushed Grayson upright again. "Do you know how much is at stake here? People are hurting, and you just walk away and have a pity party for several days? This is NOT the time for that."

"Trez, what are you doing?" I said, running towards them. But before I reached them, Grayson caused the ropes around him to untangle themselves and then latch on Trez.

"I'm here now, aren't I?" said Grayson as he grabbed the ropes across Trez's chest and held him there. "And I know what I did was wrong, so will you at least let me apologize before you start with your threats?" He pushed Trez away, and just before Trez was about to fall onto his face, the ropes suddenly dropped from him, and he regained his balance.

Trez just stood there in shock, looking at the ropes on the ground around him.

"I came here to find Wren and then call another meeting to decide what we should do. The sooner, the better," said Grayson with an air of confidence I had never seen in him before. I liked it.

Trez recalled his rope back to his side and then looked up, his shocked, angry face slowly softening as he looked at Grayson and me.

"My apologies as well," He finally said, shaking his head. "Blame it on my old habits." Trez held out his hand. Grayson took it, and they shook hands.

"I am so sorry," I awkwardly interjected. "I would stay and chat, but I really need to get back and save Root, so if you don't mind, I will be leaving now." I turned to leave, and Grayson caught my hand.

"Wait, what happened?" he asked. "Let me go with you, sorry, is that all you needed, Trez?" Trez nodded.

"Ok, great," I said, running over to my gate and unlocking it. "I'll explain everything to you on the way."

The guards who escorted me were still waiting for me with my horse. I went to jump on my horse, but Grayson stopped me.

"Wait, I can teleport us down there," he said. "It would be much quicker."

"You can what?" I asked, confused.

"Teleport, you know, like they do in that show Star Tre-"

"I know what it is," I interrupted. "I am just shocked you can do it. Why didn't you mention this before?"

Grayson shrugged and held out his hand.

"If you take my hand I can get us to the castle."

I took it, still feeling confused as to what exactly was about to happen.

"Wait!" I said, taking my hand back, "Don't take me to the castle. I need to go to my apothecary to make the potion first."

"You have a what?" he said. "Oh, never mind. I have never seen it, though, so you will have to picture it in your mind, and then I can use that to get us there. Make sure it's clear, though."

Now I started panicking. Can he also read my mind?

"Ready?" he asked, holding out his hand again.

I turned to the guards. "Um, I guess we will see you back at the castle then," I said, shrugging my shoulders. I then closed my eyes and imagined the front of my apothecary.

"Ok, ready," I said

"Great," said Grayson as he grabbed my hand. There was a loud gust of wind, and when I opened my eyes, the same image I had been imagining was now there in front of me.

"That was crazy!" I said, laughing nervously.

"I know, pretty cool, huh," he said, straightening his clothes out.

I remembered our urgency and quickly ran up to the front door and unlocked it.

Grayson followed me in and listened to me explain everything that had happened while I frantically set about grabbing supplies. Once I had what I needed, I went to work concocting the potion.

"I am impressed, Wren," said Grayson, who was now looking intently at a potion I had on one of my shelves. I looked up briefly and saw a look of pure admiration on his face. I shook my head and went back to work. I had to focus. I quickly ground up a whole flower into a fine pulp, dumped it into a small jar, threw in a pinch of fairy wing dust, added water, and sealed it up with a cork.

As soon as I was done, Grayson grabbed my hand once again, and in a second, we were standing in the castle's courtyard. I immediately took off without waiting for Grayson. Lyra looked up as I ran back into the room Root was in with tears on her face.

"The bleeding certainly slowed, and we were able to get him stitched up and bandaged, but it wasn't enough," she choked. I pushed past her and yanked the potion out of my bag. I went to dump it into Root's mouth but caught myself; remembering it had to be in the sun to reach its full potency. I noticed sunlight pouring in from a window across the room.

"Drag his bed over to that window," I yelled to Lyra and the nurse.

"But Miss, it's-" the nurse faltered.

"NOW!" I shouted as I ran towards the window and flung it open. They both jumped and pushed the bed across the room. It bumped up against the wall the window was on, and his pale face lit up in the sunlight. I held the potion in the sunlight and it instantaneously turned a deep sparkling purple. I opened Root's mouth and dumped the entire contents.

I sat back, breathing heavily, waiting. Tears sprang to my eyes. Just before I threw myself into a rage, wondering what the realms Trez had given me, Root sat straight up in bed gasping. He panicked and looked around but calmed down as soon as his eyes met mine. He grabbed me and gave me a huge hug. I laughed or cried; I couldn't tell which it was. I was just happy he was ok.

Lyra had run out of the room, and she quickly came back with Captain Tarren and Falveron. More laughter and rejoicing filled the room. Many hugs were given, and Captain Tarren didn't stop thanking me. Root began to feel so much better that he took off his bandage, which revealed a completely healed wound other than a faint scar. I marveled at how well Trez's flower had worked. Moments later Root was even up out of bed, asking his father about the fighting.

"The fighting has died down, and my men are working on clean up," said Captain Tarren. "Our guard suffered several casualties, but I am proud to say that even though several citizens were injured, all survived. My men performed bravely." He paused briefly, then cleared his throat and continued. "The dwarves made a clean getaway, but we were able to capture one dwarf that we are currently keeping in the dungeon. We have been questioning him, but the only thing he has told us is that King Dorgan will not stop these attacks until there are enough gate key gemstones for all his people and that he was insulted by the measly fourteen gemstones we had sent him from before. With that being said, it seems that we now find ourselves in an all-out war."

The conversation continued, but I stopped listening. I was suddenly overwhelmed by the feeling of absolute failure. This was my realm, which seemed perfectly fine when I had initially arrived a year ago, but now it was crumbling around me. On top of that, it was only the first attack, and Root had almost died. I couldn't help but feel this was completely my fault.

"Wren, are you ok?" Root said, interrupting my thoughts.

"Oh, yes," I said, trying to conceal the fact that my mental state was on the edge of spiraling wildly out of control. Root looked at me as if he didn't believe me. He came up to me and hugged me. I was just about to burst into tears when I heard Grayson's voice coming from the door.

"Glad to see you're ok." I quickly turned around out of Root's hug to look at Grayson, who was surprisingly smiling. "Wren was so worried about you. Glad we made it in time." He came up and held out his hand for Root to shake it. Root hesitated.

"Root, Grayson was the one who got me here in time. Without him, I am not sure we would have made it." I said.

"Well," sighed Root. "In that case, I am sincerely grateful to you, Grayson." He took Grayson's hand and shook it.

"And I as well," said Captain Tarren, coming up behind Grayson and patting him on the back.

"Yes, thank you, Grayson," said Falveron, joining us. "Now, I hate to rush things, but Root, if you are up to it, and since we are all here, I would like to discuss our next course of action. And Grayson, you, of course, are invited too."

I suddenly remembered that Grayson and I also had

very pressing gatekeeper matters to attend to. We both looked at each other at the same time, our brains thinking the same thing.

"It's ok, Wren, this is important. We can leave whenever you're ready," said Grayson. I nodded.

"What's going on?" asked Root.

"I actually have some urgent issues of my own that I need to share with you all as well," I said.

"Then yes, let's discuss it. I am feeling fine," said Root, stretching.

"It's settled. Let's make our way to the meeting room, shall we?" said Falveron.

We all shuffled out of the room and walked down the long hallway to where the great hall was. Grayson fell back behind the group of us, which I felt was odd for him. And then, when we made it to the meeting table, he sat across the table with Captain Tarren instead of with Root and me. I shrugged it off, and we immediately launched into all the details of what happened with Ryker.

Chapter
21

"So let me get this straight, gatekeeper Fynne can't get into his realm because it's been locked, and this Ryker fellow is demanding that Grayson give him a stone that could potentially destroy realms?" said Falveron after Grayson and I shared what had happened.

"Yes," I said.

Falveron sighed and sat back in his chair.

"I am so sorry to dump this all on you, but you needed to know. We plan on leaving as soon as possible to figure this out with the other gatekeepers."

"Completely understandable," said Falveron. "Thank you for telling me. Let's quickly discuss the issue at hand here in our realm, and then I will let you go."

"Sounds good," I said. I sat and listened as Falveron,

Captain Tarren, and Root threw around ideas on protecting the citizens and getting the dwarf king to stand down. War wasn't something we were necessarily prepared for because war had never happened in our realm as far as I knew. Captain Tarren was concerned that he didn't have enough men to protect the entire city of Luma and even brought up asking the elf queen from Misthold for help. I sat there getting frustrated, not having anything to contribute, when all of a sudden, an idea hit me.

"What if we got everyone out of the realm?"

The table became quiet, and everyone looked at me.

"Are you serious, Wren?" asked Root.

"Well, that would be the easiest way to eliminate the threat and keep everyone safe."

More silence.

"Then what?" asked Captain Tarren. "Where would they all stay? Is there a safe place they could all go to?"

I realized I hadn't thought that far. Finding housing for that many people would basically be impossible.

Grayson looked like he was going to say something, but then he stopped himself.

"Sorry," I finally said. "I didn't think that far ahead. It's just the quickest way to keep everyone safe. Root almost died today!" I practically yelled, my eyes welling up.

"But Wren, look, I am fine, it's going to be ok," said Root trying to comfort me. "I understand your thinking, but I am sure there is another way to work this all out. Leaving is an option, but I think it should be our absolute last resort," said Root.

"I agree with Root." said Falveron. "I think getting the elves help is a great start, so let's explore that."

Captain Tarren and Root both nodded.

"On that note, Wren, I know you have urgent matters to attend, so I won't keep you. And please don't worry, we will get this all sorted out." I nodded, and Root stood up, his chair scraping loudly against the floor.

"I'll see you out," said Root, pulling out my chair for me. He escorted Grayson and me out of the great hall and down the long hallway to the front courtyard.

"I will help get the horses ready," said Root, turning towards the stables. "I can ride with you both up there and then-"

"Well, actually, Grayson can teleport the both of us up there. That is how we got here so quickly."

"Oh, right, you had mentioned that," said Root, who stopped walking. "What exactly is teleporting?" he asked, turning around to face us.

"I can magically make us appear anywhere I wish," said Grayson.

"Oh," said Root, looking down at his shoes.

"Well, you ready to go then?" asked Grayson, holding out his hand to me.

"Yes, I think... Oh, wait, I forgot my satchel back in the

room Root was in. Let me go get it really quick," I said as I took off running back towards the castle.

"Wren, don't worry, I'll go get it for you," said Grayson, passing me before I could object.

Silence filled the courtyard as Grayson vanished inside the castle.

"Wren?" came from Root's voice from behind me. I took a deep breath and turned around. He was staring at me intently.

"Could you ever see yourself with me?" he asked, taking a step closer to me.

The question was blunt and shocking, but deep down, I had known this conversation would come even though I ignored it. I took a deep breath, and I did exactly as Root said. I closed my eyes and tried picturing myself with him. But instead of seeing myself relaxing with him in his treehouse, or exploring our realm, or going on walks through the forest with Neara, I saw Grayson walking me back to my car, smiling his rare smile, amusing himself with his random movie quotes. I opened my eyes again. "Root," I began. "If today has taught me anything, it's that I do love you, but not in the way you want me to. You are like family to me, and almost losing you today nearly broke me. But that is where it stops."

Root was looking down, pushing dirt around with his shoe.

"I know," he finally said. "Deep down, I knew, but there was always hope. So if you don't feel that way about me after today, then I respect that." He walked right up to me, leaned over, and kissed me on the cheek. "But please know I'll always love you," he whispered. He straightened back up and then looked back towards the castle entrance, his face shifting into a dead stare. I turned around, and Grayson was watching us with my satchel in his hands.

Grayson pointed back at the castle. "Sorry, I can just-"

"No, it's fine, we were done talking," said Root, taking a step back from me.

"Root, I-" I felt like I owed him more of an explanation than what I gave, but he cut me off.

"It's fine, Wren," he said quietly as Grayson walked up.

"Alright, ready then?" asked Grayson.

"Yes," I sighed.

"Ok then, here we go," said Grayson after an awkward moment. "And Root, I am glad you are ok. Good luck with everything, and don't worry, I'll keep her safe." Grayson reached out his hand to Root, and Root shook it.

"You better," laughed Root as if the conversation we just had never happened.

"Bye, Root," I said timidly as Grayson took my hand.

"Goodbye, Wren."

I watched as Root disappeared in a rush of wind.

Grayson quickly dropped my hand as soon as we arrived

at my gate and walked towards it.

"I messaged everyone when I went to get your satchel, and we are going to meet in Via's realm," he said, not looking at me.

My heart sank, wondering why he was acting so distant. It was probably because of Root but was that it? What if all this time he actually wasn't interested in me at all? Should I tell him how I felt? But now was kind of a bad time, we had a meeting to go to.

"Wren, are you coming?" he said, turning around.

"Oh, yes," I said as I jumped into motion. I walked past him and put my hand on the cool stone of the gateway. I tried collecting my thoughts but performing magic in a distracted brain is almost impossible. Grayson noticed I was struggling.

"Wren, calm down. What's wrong?" He asked.

I let out a deep sigh letting my hand drop from the gateway.

"Sorry," I mumbled. "I just have a lot on my mind."

"I see," said Grayson. I saw his hand from the corner of my eye rise as if he was about to place it on my back, but then he stopped and it dropped back down.

"Grayson," I said, suddenly determined. "There is something I want to-"

"Oh, wait," he said, abruptly pointing at his wrist. His gatekeeper's stone was now the color of Via's realm, meaning he was receiving a message from her. He listened to it and then sent another message back. "Sorry, can it wait? Via said people have already started arriving so we have to go."

"Uh, yes, sure," I said. Clearly, he did not want to have this conversation now. I gathered my thoughts enough to open my gate, and before I knew it, I found myself climbing up the stairs to Via's clock tower.

Chapter 23

"Alright, looks like everyone is here except for Kygra," said Grayson as we settled into our seats amongst the random chairs and boxes scattered around Via's loft. "I messaged her but heard no resp-" He winced and covered his ears, the gatekeeper's stone on his wrist now light green. It was a long moment before it turned back to its normal deep red.

"Well, sounds like she is finally here," he moaned, rubbing his head. "Via, can you go let her in?"

"Aye, aye, captain," said Via as she jumped up and took the fire pole down to her gate. I looked over at Trez, considering Via just spurted out pirate lingo. He looked slightly offended, which made me smile.

Grayson was still rubbing his head. "I need to tell that dragon she doesn't need to yell when she sends these messages."

"Hello, little mouse," came Kygra's voice from down below. " Leah, was it? No? Oh, Via. Right!" Kygra noisily made her way up the stairs, and soon her head popped up. "Hi everyone, sorry I'm late," she said as she shuffled past everyone trying to find a seat.

"Kygra, glad you could make it," said Grayson. "How are things in your realm?"

"Oh, just great," said Kygra, getting to one corner of the room but still not finding a place to sit. "I took it back over, so that was good. But let me tell you, it was not pretty. Still isn't, but it's better, I think.. you know?"

Nobody responded.

Via giggled, clearly amused. "Kygra, come sit by me," Via motioned towards an empty chair near where we were sitting, which unfortunately was on the other side of the room.

"Oh, thank you, don't mind if I do," said Kygra, turning around and bumping into everyone once again as she made her way back. She came to a stop in front of Trez.

"Oh wait, silly me!" she exclaimed, smacking her palm on her head. In a poof that blew Trez's hat off, she turned into a bird and flew over to the empty chair, where she hovered for a moment. Then, with a loud thud, she turned herself back into a human and plopped down directly on the chair. Everyone was staring at her.

"Sorry, continue," she said, leaning over and resting her chin in her hand. Trez angrily put his hat back on. Via giggled again and took her seat too.

"Ok," sighed Grayson. He seemed nervous as he stepped up on a crate next to Via to address us all. "Now that we are all here, I would first like to apologize to everyone who was there the day Ryker attacked."

Via jerked her head up to look at him and then looked at me. She mouthed the word "wow" and gave me a thumbs up. I just shook my head and went back to watching him, not wanting to make a scene. But secretly, I was just as excited as Via to be witnessing this new and improved Grayson.

"I am sorry that I ran off and ignored all your messages," continued Grayson. "I was overwhelmed and not sure what to do. But I realized that hiding was not beneficial to anyone, and I wanted to help make things right. Especially for you, Fynne, I can't even begin to imagine what you are going through."

Fynne nodded his head and murmured his approval.

"With that being said, let me catch you all up on what exactly happened the other day."

Grayson launched into all the details and even allowed me to share what was going on in my realm. He then also explained every detail about the dark stones he was protecting. I can't believe he actually took my advice and was being open about everything. I felt proud but stuffed it down, trying not to get my hopes up about him, considering I now wasn't sure how he felt about me anymore.

"In conclusion, our main decision we have to make is

what we do about Ryker's request," said Grayson once he was done explaining. "Fynne, have you been able to separate the stones?"

Fynne leaned forward in his chair. "No," he said, rubbing his face, "Nothing works. The woman who forced me to join the stones together had told me they were now inseparable unless we had the heart of the light stone. After trying everything, I am starting to believe her."

"Do you have it with you?" asked Launch.

"Yes, right here," said Fynne, taking it out of his pocket. Launch took it and inspected it.

"You said that the dark stones are essentially the opposite of the light stones, correct?" asked Launch, now poking it with a strange tool he had pulled from his pocket.

"Yes," replied Grayson

"Well, in that case, I believe the stones are so equal in magic and non-magic that they basically cancel each other out. I have things that I could try, but I would be afraid of cracking or chipping them as I did with mine. You would need a greater power far beyond anything I have to separate them."

Fynne groaned. "Then what are our options then?" he asked, frustrated. "I need to get back to my family, and I am willing to do anything. What is the worst that could happen if we just give Ryker the heart of the dark stone?"

Grayson sighed. "From my understanding, the heart of the dark stone can destroy realms. Not just close them like the smaller dark stones did with your realm Fynne, but completely destroy them." Silence filled the room.

"Is that Ryker's goal, though?" Said Trez. Everyone looked at him. "Just think it through. He has been messing with us this whole time, and I feel like, with the knowledge and power he has, he could have easily caused a lot more issues than this."

"You're right," said Jumana, who had been completely silent up to this point. "From my reasoning, I believe that he is pushing you all to find Linore because he wants to find Linore and, for some reason, can't do it without all of you."

"Then what does he want with Linore?" asked Fynne.

Grayson sighed. "Well, when Ryker originally asked me to help him, he told me that he wants to send magic back to where it belongs, which is back through Linore's gate."

"But what does that mean for us in the realms?" said Isla, after a moment's pause. "Where would we live? Our lives would be completely uprooted."

"Whoa, whoa," said Fynne, "Can we just concentrate on the issue at hand? We can work through all that later. Right now, I just need my family back."

"Agreed," said Trez. "So the real question is if we give Ryker the heart of the dark stone, then what's to stop him from destroying realms? Or does he just want to defeat Linore?"

"That I do not know," said Grayson.

"Ok, then let's say we give Ryker the heart of the dark

stone," said Fynne. "Couldn't we guard our gates until we find Linore?"

"I could do that," said Kygra. "I could just become a dragon and sit watch in the gate circle. Also, I am very strong, can stay awake for days, and I can blow fire."

"There you go," said Fynne. "Let's just do that!"

Everyone looked skeptical.

"Look," sighed Fynne, "I need to get my family back. The only way I have back is finding Linore. If there is even a small hope of Ryker knowing where she is I will do anything to get that information from him." Fynne emphasized the word "anything" while looking directly at Grayson.

"Jumana," said Grayson, still looking at Fynne. "What do you think?"

"At this point, the quickest way to find Linore would be to give Ryker the heart of the dark stone. I also believe that Ryker's fight is not against us and our realms but against Linore. With that being said, I also agree that we should still protect our gates just in case. I have no problem with Kygra being there to protect our realms, especially if she is willing to do it. So I agree with Fynne."

"That's enough for me then," said Grayson. "Anyone else have any objections?"

No one said anything. I mean, who could argue against the woman who ran the realm of wisdom?

"It's settled then," said Grayson. "I will message Ryker to

meet me outside his gate. Kygra, I would like you to come with me, and then from that point on, I will need you to be guarding the gate circle. We can switch on and off for breaks."

"I can help guard," said Fynne.

"Me too," said Trez.

"Perfect," said Grayson.

"I am also coming with you when you meet Ryker," said Trez.

Grayson paused, scratching his head. "I don't think that would be a great idea."

"Why not?" demanded Trez.

"There is a lot at stake here, and with how you reacted last time, I am just not sure that it would be a good idea."

After a moment's pause, Trez stood down.

"Alright," he said. "But someday I will face him."

"Sounds great," said Grayson.

Trez sat back down in his chair in a huff.

"Ok, then," said Grayson. "Kygra, are you ok with starting your watch now?"

"Yup," said Kygra, jumping up from her chair. "My realm can handle being without me for a few days."

"Great, and as we said, we can jump in and help too if needed."

"Perfect," said Kygra.

"Alright, let's do this," said Grayson.

Grayson sent the message. Moments later, his

gatekeeper's stone turned the light pinkish purplish color of realm eleven.

"We are good to go. He can meet us right now," said Grayson, turning to Kygra. "Ready?" he asked.

"Ready as I'll ever be," said Kygra, running to the fire pole and sliding down, followed by Via so she could unlock the gate for them. Grayson hesitated but ultimately made his way towards the fire pole as well.

"Grayson, wait!" I suddenly yelled. Everyone that was left looked over at me, and I could feel my face burning. "Just be safe," I finally said. He looked as if he was about to step towards me but changed his mind.

"I will," he said, grabbing the pole and sliding down after the others.

Chapter 24

Other than the sound of Trez fidgeting in his chair, the room was filled with intense silence, everyone waiting for the sound of Via opening the gate back up for Grayson to come back. Time seemed to pass so slowly, but it was only about ten minutes before Grayson burst back through the gate. I briefly heard him talk to Via, and then they both raced up the stairs.

"How did it go?" asked Fynne, getting up from his seat.

"It went fine," said Grayson, "nothing out of the ordinary."

"Where is Linore?" asked Trez, who had also gotten up from his seat.

"In the void," said Grayson. You could cut the silence with a knife.

"Interesting," said Launch.

"Is that all he said?" asked Fynne after a moment.

"Yes," sighed Grayson, "But he said that if his insight was correct, we have everything we need to find her." Grayson looked at Launch.

"But wait, didn't you say it was going to take you months to get your ship back up and running?" I asked. Everyone murmured their own concerns.

"Actually," said Launch, "Via and I have been working on some things and we could potentially be ready to leave by tomorrow." The room once again fell silent.

"Are you serious?" asked Grayson. "How?"

"Well," said Launch, "Turns out Via's power can charge a sunstone."

"It's true!" said Via. "Watch!" She ran over to one of her desks in the corner, opened a drawer, and pulled out a round yellow stone. She closed her eyes, and a bright light slowly started to build in the palm of her hand. The light filled up the stone, its edges creeping up the sphere. Just as light completely enveloped the stone, a bright flash filled the room, followed by a rush of wind, causing everyone to close their eyes. Via's panting filled the now completely silent room. I slowly opened my eyes and there, in Via's open hand, was now a glowing sunstone.

And that is where my side of the story ends...

Before you get upset over this fact, may I please remind you that I warned you fairly. But beginnings have middles, and questions have answers. With that being said, I have recruited the help of my fellow gatekeepers, all twelve of them, in fact, to help me finish this story while also sharing their own perspectives. Considering where I have ended my story and also the fact that his is the next gate in line, Launch will be writing the next installment of our gatekeeper chronicles. He may seem quiet and reserved but believe me, there is much more to him than meets the eye. I leave you in his capable hands.

I wish you well, and may you find the true meaning of magic along this journey.

TikTok:
@thegatekeepersshop

Shop:
www.thegatekeepersshop.com

Contact:
thegateekeepersshop@gmail.com